MARGARET MANCHESTER

Edward Earle

To my sons
Richard and Stephen
With love

Acknowledgement

Thank you to my husband, Alec, for being my sounding board while I wrote this book, for his patience, understanding and support, and for providing feedback throughout the process. I could not have completed it without his assistance.

I am very grateful to my sister, Linda Brown, and my father-in-law, Leslie Manchester for reading and commenting on my final draft before publication.

The cover artwork was designed by the author and prepared for publication by Alec Manchester.

Chapter 1

Edward Earle sat before a roaring log fire, playing Whist for halfpennies. His friend, Tommy, was winning—a pile of coins was stacked on his side of the table, and he wore a massive grin.

Without warning, the door to the cottage was flung open, and four constables burst into the room.

Tommy jumped up from his seat, his mouth agape and eyes wide.

'Edward Earle?' asked the eldest constable, looking from one man to the other.

'I'm Edward Earle, sir,' said Edward, sitting back in his chair and crossing his long legs in front of him. 'Please state your business.'

'Ah! So, this must be Thomas Bell, your accomplice,' said the constable, looking from Edward to Tommy, who stood with his head lowered, sweat beading on his brow.

'My accomplice?' Edward's heart beat quickly, but his face showed no fear. With his brows furrowed, he said, 'Tommy is my friend and landlord. Nothing more.'

1

'We have reason to believe that you and your so-called friend and landlord, or whatever else he might be, happen to be highway robbers.'

'Sir, you are mistaken.' Edward put his cards on the table, face down as though he intended to continue the game, and then standing up tall and straight, he faced the constable. 'What reason do you have to believe that?'

'A witness gave us your names. She told us where to find you, an' all. Fancy that! Tellin' a woman your real name and where you live. Foolish that was.'

The old constable laughed loudly at the young men's naivety in trusting a woman, and the other policemen failed to hide their smirks.

Edward's face remained impassive, but inside, he was fuming.

Who could have betrayed us?

'What have you got to say for yourselves?' asked the older constable.

'You have the wrong men,' said Edward in the most haughty voice he could muster. 'I have no idea why you believe my friend and I are highway robbers. I think someone has played a joke on you and sent you on a wild goose chase.'

Edward surprised himself at how calm and reasoned he sounded.

'What's your line of work?' asked the constable, raising an eyebrow.

'I work as a clerk for Mr Travis, a solicitor in Silksworth. He'll vouch for me.'

'That accounts for his pompous voice,' said one of the younger constables, rolling his eyes.

'I'm a woodcutter,' offered Tommy. 'There's not much else

to do around here.'

Edward silently congratulated Tommy. There was wood crackling in the grate, a stack by the hearth, and a well-stocked wood store by the door that the policemen would have passed on their way in. His explanation sounded very plausible. Very plausible indeed.

The two constables who appeared to be in charge went outside for a few minutes, and when they returned, the elder one said, 'Edward Earle and Thomas Bell, we are arrestin' you both on suspicion of highway robbery. You are to come with us to Durham and you'll be held in Durham Gaol until we get to the bottom of this.'

Edward glanced at Tommy and saw the panic growing in his friend's eyes.

'An announcement will be placed in the newspaper,' continued the policeman, 'and if anyone can identify either one of you as highwaymen, you will be charged and stand trial. Do you understand?'

'Yes, we understand,' said Edward. 'But I can assure you that you're making a huge mistake. We are not the men you seek.'

Tommy pushed a constable out of his way and rushed for the door. He ran outside and entered the dense woodland that surrounded the cottage.

Three men gave chase and disappeared into the night whilst the eldest stayed with Edward.

'Funny he should run away like that if he's innocent like you say.' The shrewd policeman watched for Edward's reaction.

'We are both innocent,' Edward replied. 'Tommy's just scared of being locked up, that's all.'

'Ah! So, he's been in gaol before, has he?' The constable's eyes shone with glee.

3

'No,' said Edward firmly. 'Not a gaol as such. An orphanage.'

The constable didn't reply, and Edward understood that to mean he was aware of the conditions in which orphaned children were kept and the cruelty they endured while supposedly being cared for.

They stood in silence as they watched Tommy being dragged back into the cottage.

'Don't lock me up! Please, don't lock me up!' begged Tommy.

'Give over, lad,' said the elder constable. 'Calm yourself down. If it bothers you that much, we'll put you in a cell with your mate here.'

'Breathe, Tommy,' said Edward. 'You heard the man. You won't be alone, and it won't be for long, I promise. They'll soon realise their mistake and let us out.'

Tommy looked at Edward and gave a slight nod, still breathing rapidly.

The youngest policeman handcuffed Edward, and when Tommy held out his arms in front of him, showing a hand and a stump, he asked, 'How can I handcuff this one if he doesn't have a hand?'

'Take them out to the cart and shackle their feet together.'

Edward and Tommy were ushered into the cart by the two younger constables, one of whom locked the shackles around their ankles, and then the policemen sat on either side of their prisoners.

The older men remained in the cottage for a while, and Edward presumed they must be searching for anything that could be used as evidence against them—weapons, clothing or stolen goods, but they returned to the cart empty-handed, sat up front, and the cart lurched forward on the soft ground.

Edward released the breath that he'd been holding.

As they travelled to Durham, thoughts of betrayal weighed heavily on Edward's mind. Few people knew he was a highwayman, and even fewer knew where he lived, and he pondered which one of the people he trusted had given him up to the authorities.

After some time, he realised he was wasting time thinking about who was responsible for their capture when he should be working out how he and Tommy could escape—they couldn't risk staying in gaol because it would only take one person to say they were highway robbers, truthfully or maliciously, and they'd be convicted and hanged for the crime.

As they were in handcuffs and shackles and outnumbered two to one, they had no chance of getting away from the police on the journey to Durham. Edward decided he would have to be patient and wait for an opportunity to arise. He looked up at the starry sky and closed his eyes. *Please, God, let us survive this.* He then chided himself for reverting to prayer after such a long time, thinking himself a hypocrite.

When they reached Durham, the cart climbed a steep hill and was driven through a large pair of wooden gates, which closed behind them with a thud. The constables pushed Edward and Tommy off the back of the cart, and they landed heavily on the cobbled ground. They then pulled the men to their feet and manhandled them into a dark building and down a stone staircase, the iron shackles digging into their flesh as they walked.

As soon as he entered the gaol, the overwhelming stench of stale sweat, urine and excrement filled Edward's nostrils and made him want to retch. The cells they passed had upright iron bars, with men and women peering through them, unkempt and malnourished. When they reached the first empty cell, the gaoler opened the door, and the two young constables pushed the prisoners inside, removed their handcuffs and shackles, and then left hastily, holding their noses.

Water dripped from the ceiling, ran down the walls, and pooled on the floor. Rats ran up and down the passageway, occasionally stopping and sniffing the air, trying to locate any leftover food. Judging by the emaciated prisoners he'd seen, Edward didn't think they'd have much success.

'Are you alright, Tommy?' Edward asked, putting his hand on his friend's shoulder.

'I'll have a bruise the size of Newcastle on me backside tomorrow,' said Tommy with a straight face.

Edward laughed loudly, and the sound echoed around the prison. No matter how dire the circumstances, Tommy could always make him laugh.

'Shut up, will ya? Some of us are tryin' to sleep,' shouted a prisoner.

'We should get some sleep,' whispered Edward. 'It must be well past midnight by now.'

There was only one bed in the cold, underground cell, and the two men lay back to back for warmth.

Edward didn't sleep well, disturbed by thoughts and fears in his overactive mind, as well as the unfamiliar noises of the prisoners coughing, crying and snoring throughout the night.

He recalled that he'd once said to Tommy that they should never get caught, and he was furious because they should never have been caught; they had been so careful. Someone they trusted had betrayed them, and once again, he considered those who could have been responsible and wondered why they'd done it. Eventually, he drifted into a dreamless sleep.

The following day, the men were woken by a gaoler bringing their breakfasts. He opened the cell door, placed a tray with two small bowls of gruel and a jug of water on the floor, and quickly retreated, locking the door behind him.

The food looked so disgusting that Edward was inclined to refuse it, but he forced himself to eat the tasteless, lumpy mixture, knowing he needed to keep up his strength if he wanted to escape; some of the prisoners he'd seen the night before would have struggled to walk across the yard, never mind make a run for it. After eating and drinking, Edward stretched and flexed his muscles to alleviate the tension in them and also, in an attempt to stay fit—he had to stay strong to stand any chance of getting out of there.

The day dragged on and seemed to be endless. Edward and Tommy had little to say to each other for fear of being overheard, and unused to captivity, they paced the small cell, which was four steps long and two steps wide.

Around midday, the same gaoler brought them a bowl of fatty meat stew and a piece of bread each, and late in the afternoon, they had the same meal again, only the bread was stale by then.

With nothing else to do that evening, Edward sat on the bed, his back against the cold, damp wall, and wondered how he, Edward Earle, who had left Rookhope as a small boy, had ended up in this perilous place with the threat of a noose hanging over him.

Chapter 2

'Mrs Robson! Mrs Robson!'

Edward Earle ran into the farmhouse kitchen, breathing heavily.

'Me mother's sick,' he said. 'Can you come over to our house and make her better?'

'What's the matter with her?' asked Mrs Robson, who was seated by the unlit fire, knitting tiny clothes for her eleventh baby, whose arrival was expected in just a few weeks.

'She says her head hurts. She's holdin' it like this.' He put his hands on each side of his head and screwed up his face. 'She's sweatin' a lot an' all, and she has spots all over her.'

Mrs Robson's eyes widened at his description of his mother's ailments.

'John!' she said to her son, who had followed Edward into the house. 'Go and find your father. He'll likely be in the barn or the byre. Tell him to fetch the doctor for Mary Earle. Hurry now!'

John turned and ran out of the house, and Edward walked towards the door to follow his friend.

'You should stay here, Ed,' said Mrs Robson.

'Why?' asked Edward. 'I told me mother I'd go straight home. I might get into trouble if I don't.'

'You'll not get into trouble, lad. Why don't you stay here and play with our John for a while when he gets back? Alright?'

Edward nodded his head and sat on the proddy mat by Mrs Robson's feet with two of John's little brothers and his sister, Dorothy, who held his hand while he waited for John to return. After John, Dorothy was his next best friend.

Mr Robson barged into the kitchen and demanded, 'What's goin' on? The cow's about to calve.'

'The lad said his mother's covered in spots,' said Mrs Robson. 'And she's got a fever.'

'Oh, hell!' said Mr Robson. 'The cow will have to manage on her own. I'll saddle up and go down to the village.'

Edward looked up at Mrs Robson, wondering why Mr Robson had said a curse word and left in such a hurry. *Was his mother very poorly?* He was pleased Dorothy was still holding his hand, or he might have cried.

'It'll be alright, Ed,' said Mrs Robson in a reassuring tone. 'Don't you worry about your mother. She'll be fine.'

Edward played with his friends, John and Dorothy, all day and had tea with them. While the children were eating at the table, Mr Robson came home and took off his hat, and Edward thought he looked sad.

'Bessie, will you come outside for a minute?' he asked his wife.

Mrs Robson got up from her chair and shuffled her heavily pregnant body towards the door. Edward knew they would be talking about his mother, so he left the table and followed them.

9

From the doorway, he heard Mr Robson say, '—typhus fever. She's bad with it, real bad. The doctor doesn't think she'll make it.'

'She won't make what?' asked Edward.

Mrs Robson put her hand to her mouth and said, 'Dear God! You shouldn't listen to people talkin', Ed. It'll get you into bother.'

'Give ower, Bessie. Now's not the time to scold the lad.' Taking Edward's hand, Mr Robson said, 'Come ower here, lad. There's somethin' I need to tell ya.'

Mr Robson sat Edward on a tree stump at the edge of the farmyard, and he knelt in front of the boy. 'You know, sometimes when people get sick, they die,' said Mr Robson.

Edward nodded. 'Our teacher at school got sick and she died.'

'Aye, that's right. Miss Robinson. She did. Well, your mother's sick, Ed. Very sick. An' there's a chance that she might die.'

Edward looked at Mr Robson, and his bottom lip wobbled. 'But what if she does? What will happen to me?'

'Don't worry about that, Ed. We'll pray that she gets better. The doctor is stayin' with her tonight so she's in good hands. If anyone can save her, it's him.'

A single tear rolled down Edward's plump cheek. 'Can I stay here?' he asked.

Mr Robson looked down and said, 'I'll tell you what, lad. You can stay with us until your mother's well enough to look after you again. How does that sound?'

Edward smiled. He was excited to stay with John and Dorothy and be part of their large family, even if it was just for a short while until his mother got better, and he ran back into the house to finish his tea.

The following day, Edward, John and Dorothy were playing hide and seek in the farmyard when the doctor walked through the gate. He stood in front of the children and removed his hat.

'Is your father at home?' he asked John.

'Aye, he's in the barn with the new calf,' replied John, and he ran to the barn to fetch him.

The farmhouse door opened, and Mrs Robson filled the doorway, her welcoming smile fading when she saw the doctor's countenance.

Mr Robson strode across the yard and shook the doctor's hand. They spoke quietly, and although Edward couldn't hear what they said, he knew they were talking about him because Mr Robson gestured towards him. The doctor nodded and wandered away down the fields toward the village.

Mr Robson took Edward's hand and led him back to the tree stump where he'd sat the day before and sat him down.

'There's no easy way to say this, lad,' said Mr Robson. 'The doctor did everythin' he could for your mother but she died this mornin'.'

Edward sat looking up at Mr Robson, and when the news sunk in, tears filled his eyes, and he began to sob. Mr Robson knelt on the grass and put his arms around the boy to comfort him, and Edward clung to him.

He was distraught. He had loved his mother, and he was more upset than he'd ever been before in his life. In his mind, he pictured her smiling face and imagined hearing her soft voice and feeling her loving touch.

Through his grief, the words Mr Robson had spoken the day before entered Edward's mind. He'd said Edward could stay at the farm until his mother was well enough to look after him again, but she couldn't look after him any more because she was dead. So, surely, that must mean he could stay at the Robsons' farm forever and live with John and Dorothy. He felt excited at the prospect of having lots of brothers and sisters. Mr Robson would be his father—that would be nice because Mr Robson was a kind man and he'd never had a father before—and Mrs Robson would be his new mother.

When Edward stopped crying, Mr Robson wiped his face with a cotton handkerchief, held it up to his nose, and told him to blow into it.

My mother used to do that.

Tears threatened to fall again, and Edward sniffed loudly.

'There's somethin' I need to ask you, Ed,' said Mr Robson. 'Did your mother ever tell you who your father was?'

'No, she said I never had a father.'

For a split second, Mr Robson looked slightly amused at the boy's innocence, but his face straightened just as quickly, and he said, 'Last night, your mother told the doctor about your father. Turns out he's a man called Malham and he lives near Durham. We'll go and see him later this week, after the funeral.'

'I don't know him. I don't want to go,' pleaded the boy. 'I want to stay here with you.'

'I'm afraid you can't stay here, Ed. There isn't room. The house is overcrowded already and Mrs Robson's goin' to have another baby soon.'

'I could stay in the barn,' suggested Edward. 'I've slept in there before with your John.'

'Aye, you could, I suppose,' said Mr Robson, looking upwards and moving his hand to his chin. 'It's not unpleasant in the summer if you don't mind sharin' it with the mice and the rats and the bats, but you'd freeze to death in there when the winter comes.'

Edward was horrified at the possibility of freezing to death in Mr Robson's barn. He'd never considered what it would be like to stay there during a Weardale winter when the snow was often deep enough to cover the houses and the winds strong enough to blow him off his feet.

'We'll go and see your father on Saturday,' said Mr Robson. 'He'll know what should be done.'

Mr Robson walked away, leaving Edward sitting on the tree stump. Tears poured down the boy's cheeks. Losing his mother and being refused a place in the Robsons' home was too much for him to bear.

Chapter 3

Granby Hall, Durham
August 1757

Two days after his mother's funeral, Mrs Robson woke Edward at the break of dawn.

'Come along, Ed,' she said. 'We have to get you ready to meet your father today.'

Bleary-eyed and with hay sticking out of his hair, Edward followed her from the barn to the house, where he saw a jug and bowl on the table, along with a bar of soap.

'I don't need a wash, Mrs Robson. I had one not long ago,' said Edward, backing away from her.

'You're havin' one,' she reached out to grab his arm, but he moved further away. 'You have to look your best for your father.'

'I don't have a father!'

Mr Robson came through the door, and Edward ran to him and wrapped his arms around the man's legs.

'He's refusing to have a wash,' said Mrs Robson, holding a hand to her belly. 'I can't be bothered with this. I've got ten of me own to see to and another one comin' any day.'

'You get on with breakfast, Bessie,' said Mr Robson. 'I'll see to the lad.'

After some coaxing, Mr Robson persuaded Edward to undress, wash with a cloth, and dry himself with a piece of linen, and then he brushed the hay, dust and tangles out of the boy's long, dark hair.

'Should his hair be tied back, do you think?' Mr Robson asked his wife, who was stirring a large pan of creamy porridge.

'Aye, it should. It'll look messy otherwise, especially if the wind gets up. There's a black ribbon of our Dorothy's in the top drawer.'

Mr Robson opened the top drawer of the chest and pulled out a black ribbon. He brushed Edward's hair back and tied it neatly at the nape of his neck.'

Mrs Robson had washed Edward's Sunday clothes and left them folded on a chair. When he put them on, she asked, 'Where has little Ed gone? I don't recognise this smart young man standin' here.'

Edward blushed at the compliment but smiled back at her.

The journey from Weardale to Durham was long, hot and dusty, with little conversation passing between Mr Robson and Edward. Sitting up front, Edward watched the landscape flatten out, the rugged, heather-covered hills giving way to a patchwork of green fields and golden crops interspersed by small villages and towns. They broke the trip by stopping briefly at Wolsingham and Willington for refreshments and to water the horse.

As they drove into Durham, Edward's eyes were wide. He was amazed by the tall, narrow houses clustered together, the sheer number of people milling about, the deafening metallic sound of horses and carts on the cobblestones, children laughing and playing in the streets, and hawkers selling their wares. They crossed two long, stone bridges before leaving the town and travelling eastwards.

Edward was relieved when they left the town behind them, and it was quieter again. It didn't seem like they had travelled far before they came to a high stone wall, and behind it stood the largest house that Edward had ever seen.

'This is Granby Hall,' said Mr Robson. 'This is where your father lives.'

Mr Robson left the horse and cart outside the wrought iron gates and strolled up the drive with Edward trailing behind.

Lord Malham and his third wife, an elegant woman in a low-necked, blue silk dress and feathered hat, were seated on the front lawn enjoying the midday sunshine. The gentleman shifted slightly when he saw a man and boy approach, and a wave of his hand sent the butler to meet them and learn their business.

When the butler returned, he said, 'Sir, Mr Robson from Weardale would like to discuss an urgent matter with you.'

'Really! I don't know the man. Did he give you his card?'

'No, my Lord. Men of his class don't carry calling cards.'

'Hmm. Well, I suppose I'd better see what he wants.' Turning to his wife, he said, 'Please excuse me, darling, this won't take long.'

Walking with long strides, the tall, lean gentleman went to the visitors who waited on the drive.

Dazzled by the sun, Edward lowered his head.

'Mr Robson, may I ask the purpose of your visit?' asked Lord Malham.

'Sir, it's rather a delicate matter,' Mr Robson cleared his throat. 'This lad's mother, Mary Earle, named you as his

16

father.'

With a stony face, the Lord looked at the child for a moment, and then he said, 'Lift your head, boy.'

Their bright green eyes met.

'His mother passed away last week,' said Mr Robson, 'and the lad's been livin' in our barn since then because we've no room for him in the house. What should be done with him?'

'I know nothing of the woman or the child. She must be mistaken—or perhaps she lied.'

'Me mother never told a lie in her life!' Edward glared at Lord Malham. 'You should say sorry for sayin' such an awful thing.'

'Such an insolent child could not have sprung from my loins. You asked what is to be done with him. He should be taken to an orphanage—that's where orphans belong—and perhaps he'll learn some manners there.'

'But, sir, he's ten years old,' said Mr Robson. 'He's old enough to work. Couldn't he be apprenticed to a tradesman? Surely, a gentleman of your standin' could put in a good word and find the lad a place.'

Lord Malham glanced back at his wife, who was watching the proceedings with interest, and then back at the boy.

'Reynolds!' he called.

When the butler reached his side, Lord Malham said, 'Arrange for this boy to be taken to the orphanage. He's to be kept there until he reaches the age of sixteen years.'

'Sixteen, my Lord? They're usually sent out to work by the time they're twelve.'

'I said sixteen and I meant sixteen. How dare you question me in front of our visitors?'

'I'm sorry, my Lord.'

17

'Will that be the orphanage in Durham?' asked Mr Robson.

'No, that's no good,' Lord Malham shifted uncomfortably. 'Durham is far too close for comfort. Sunderland, perhaps? Yes, take him to Sunderland. That will do nicely.'

'Sunderland is a long way from Weardale, sir. Too far for me and me family to visit the lad. Durham or Bishop Auckland would be more convenient. Please, sir, won't you reconsider?'

'Certainly not,' said Lord Malham crossly. 'Now, leave the boy and be on your way.'

'No!' cried Edward. 'Don't leave me here.'

Mr Robson turned away, walked down the drive and returned to the horse and cart without a backward glance.

'Please, Mr Robson,' shouted Edward, 'please, take me home with you. I promise I'll be no bother.'

Edward watched Mr Robson's horse and cart drive away from Granby Hall and disappear from view. Tears poured down his cheeks. He'd just lost his mother, and now, it felt like he was losing a father, too, for Mr Robson was the only father figure he'd had in his life. Edward had hoped Mr Robson would become his father and that he would be part of his family, but that could never happen now.

He had always longed for a family. When he was growing up, there had only been him and his mother in their tiny cottage, and he'd been envious of the other children at school who had proper families, with a father and mother and brothers or sisters to play with.

He looked up at the stranger standing in front of him. His mother had said this man was his father, but he didn't know him, and the man was going to send him away to a place called Sunderland, which must be a long way away if the Robsons couldn't visit him there.

His father didn't want him. The Robsons didn't want him. Nobody wanted him. Quick as a flash, the instinct to run away from this wicked man kicked in, and Edward fled towards the road as quickly as his short legs would allow.

Lord Malham swiftly ran after the boy and caught his arm, saying, 'No, you don't, you little rascal.' He escorted Edward back up the drive, walking so quickly that he almost dragged the boy behind him.

The coachman stopped a team of four beautiful bay horses alongside them, pulling the most ornate carriage that Edward had seen. He was so fascinated by the horses and the carriage that he wasn't aware Reynolds had returned until he heard Lord Malham give him his orders.

Reynolds went back to the house and came back a few minutes later carrying a small package. He opened the carriage door and helped Edward up the steps, and once the boy was seated, the butler climbed in and sat by his side.

Edward felt like a lord riding in the carriage. It was higher than the cart, and he could see for miles as they journeyed to Sunderland. Although he enjoyed riding in the carriage, he missed his friends already. The leather seat was cushioned and bouncy, and he had to resist the urge to jump on it. If John and Dorothy had been there, they would have jumped on it with him, and the thought of them all having fun together brought a smile to his lips.

When they reached the town, the carriage travelled along several streets and stopped outside a row of tall houses. Reynolds opened the door and waited for the coachman to lower the steps before he climbed out. Edward jumped down and stumbled as he landed, almost colliding with a gentleman passing by.

'Steady on, young man,' said Reynolds. 'I should prefer to deliver you in one piece!'

Edward's eyes widened at the butler's harsh tone.

Reynolds lifted his stick to knock upon a large wooden door, and a stern-looking woman answered.

'Is your master at home?' enquired Reynolds.

'If by me master you mean me husband, then aye, he is.' She turned and shouted, 'Bill, there's a gentleman here to see you.'

A middle-aged man with a long, untrimmed beard came to the door. 'Who have we got here?' he asked, looking at the boy. When he spoke, his breath smelled of alcohol, and Edward involuntarily stepped back.

'Lord Malham of Granby Hall requests that this child is to be kept at this orphanage until he turns sixteen,' said Reynolds haughtily. 'He is to be tutored in reading, writing, arithmetic, and the bible.'

'Now, look here, mister. Me and me wife take in orphans out of the goodness of our hearts, but we need children that can work for their keep. How else can we be expected to feed them? And we're no teachers. Learnin' like that costs money. I think you've brought him to the wrong place.'

Edward hoped they had come to the wrong place. He didn't like the look of the man or the woman who lived here, and his mother had warned him to stay away from people who smelled of drink.

Reynolds took the package from his coat pocket and handed it to Mr Kelly, saying, 'His Lordship is very generous. There's plenty of money in there to pay for the boy's keep for the next five years and to provide him with the very best tutor.'

Mr Kelly checked the contents and raised his eyebrows. 'You're not kiddin', are you? That's serious money, that is. Of course, we'd be glad to take the lad in.'

'I suggest you do exactly as Lord Malham asks,' said Reynolds, 'because mark my words, he will be keeping a close eye on this boy.'

Edward was heartened by Reynolds' words. If Lord Malham intended to keep a close eye on him, surely that meant he believed that he was his son and would take care of him from now on.

'You, boy,' Reynolds addressed Edward. 'I know this is not an ideal situation, but it is only a temporary arrangement. Although it may not seem so to you now, five years is not such a very long time. My advice to you would be to learn all you can while you're here. It will stand you in good stead for the future.'

'Will I see you again?' asked Edward.

'I'm sorry, lad. I doubt that very much.'

Reynolds climbed back into the carriage, and Edward's bottom lip wobbled as he watched it move away. He was being abandoned in a strange place for the second time that day.

'Come inside, boy.' Mr Kelly moved aside to let Edward pass, and he closed the door behind him. As they walked along a corridor, he asked, 'What's your name?'

'Edward Earle.'

'Funny kind of a name, that. While you're staying here, we'll call you Eddie.'

Edward wrinkled his nose at the name.

I'm not Eddie from some orphanage in Sunderland; I'm Edward Earle from Rookhope, and I always will be.

He followed Mr Kelly into a room and stood stiffly just inside the doorway. As Mrs Kelly prepared him a light supper,

21

he looked around the dark, dismal parlour and watched his new guardians—or should that be guards, he wondered.

The butler had said that staying at this place was just a temporary arrangement, but so was going to prison, thought Edward and five years was a long sentence.

Chapter 4

Durham Gaol
October 1770

After a poor night's sleep, Edward opened his eyes and looked around, wondering why the prison seemed quieter than the previous day.

When Tommy saw Edward was awake, he whispered, 'There's somethin' been botherin' us. I've been thinkin' about the other night when the policemen came to our place. It's just that I've never told anybody about what we do. Have you? Or was the policeman makin' it up?'

'I haven't told anyone, Tommy.'

'So how do the police know what we did? And how did they know where to find us?' asked Tommy dubiously.

'I don't know,' said Edward, 'I'm still trying to work that out.'

'Someone must have told them.'

'I agree, someone must have told them, but who?'

Tommy shook his head and shrugged.

Edward heard the guards walking down the passageway and lowered his eyes as they passed. He overheard them talking and soon discovered that the man in the next cell had passed away overnight and wondered if that accounted for the hush in the prison. The guards carried the body, covered with a blanket, past their cell and out of the gaol, and Edward wondered if there was a burial ground in the grounds of the gaol or if the body would be taken home to be buried in the parish churchyard.

The guard who brought their food the previous day handed Edward a pack of cards through the iron bars. 'Do you want these?'

'Yes, thank you.' Edward reached out and took them.

Nodding towards the dead man's cell, the guard said, 'They were in his pocket. I would've taken them home for me bairns, but we don't know what he died of. It might be somethin' catchin'.'

Edward nodded at the man in understanding and gratitude. He had no such qualms because he knew the cards would help pass the time while he and Tommy were imprisoned.

They played three hands of Brag before the gaoler returned with their porridge for breakfast, and Edward was glad Tommy looked more settled. They ate the bland, watery food and continued playing cards for the rest of the morning.

When they stopped to eat their midday meal, Edward wondered how much longer they would be safe at the gaol. He surmised that a notice for the newspaper would probably have been prepared the day before and the article published that day, which meant that somebody could come to identify them soon. It concerned Edward greatly that he'd not yet thought of a way for him and Tommy to get out of the gaol, and time was running out.

Instead of playing cards and reminiscing, he should have spent his time planning their escape. He vowed to watch the guards more carefully, learn their routine and look for any weaknesses that they could exploit.

After finishing his meal, Tommy lay down for a nap.

Edward wasn't surprised Tommy was tired because he'd had a restless night. He'd whimpered, cried, shouted out in his sleep, and woken many times. The worst had been when Edward woke and saw Tommy desperately trying to prise apart the iron bars to get out and then sobbing like a child when he failed. It had been heartbreaking to witness, and Edward had held his friend in his arms until he calmed and went back to sleep.

Tommy's nightmares, Edward knew, resulted from his days at the orphanage, where his experiences had been worse than most and still haunted him. Being locked up in a small space, like a gaol cell, was Tommy's greatest fear.

Edward's greatest fear was a lack of control, and he was frustrated that since he had been arrested, he'd had no control over his life whatsoever. He had always liked to work to plans, and it frustrated him that he still had not thought of a plan for their escape.

He sat on the edge of the bed with his head in his hands, determined to find a way to get them out, but his mind was completely blank. Sitting and staring at the flagstone floor, he recalled the first time he had met Tommy Bell.

Chapter 5

The Orphanage, Sunderland
August 1757

The day after he arrived at the orphanage, Edward got out of bed and looked around the room. Five other boys of various ages were washing and getting dressed, so Edward did the same. A water jug stood on top of a small chest of drawers by his bed. The water was cold, and he limited the wash to his hands.

His clothes were folded neatly in the top drawer. He quickly removed his nightshirt and put them on, and then crumpled up the nightshirt, shoved it under his pillow and pulled up the bed sheet and blanket. He knew he should have folded his nightshirt like his mother had taught him, but he reckoned that nobody would see it or tell him off for it, so why should he bother?

The previous night, the boys had been sound asleep when Mrs Kelly showed Edward to his bed, and they didn't seem to notice him in the corner of the room that morning. He followed them downstairs and into the dining room for breakfast, where many more boys and girls waited for food. As he stood in the doorway, unsure what to do, the children stopped chatting and stared at him.

His heart started to pound in his chest, and he felt the urge to run away.

'Good morning, children,' said Mr Kelly, moving to Edward's side. 'A new boy joined us yesterday. This is Eddie.'

'Good morning, Eddie,' chanted the children, who seemed well-versed in welcoming new children to the orphanage.

Edward looked at them all and smiled, thinking most of them looked friendly enough, certainly more welcoming than Mr and Mrs Kelly had been the day before. It might not be so bad here, after all, he thought optimistically.

'There's a seat at that table over there, Eddie, next to Tommy,' said Mr Kelly, pointing at an empty chair. 'Go and sit down quickly. The girls are about to serve breakfast.'

Edward sat beside a boy who looked too big to be in a children's home.

'Morning, Eddie,' said the boy. 'I'm Tommy Bell. Don't look so worried. I'll look out for you.'

'Thank you,' said Edward, 'But me name's Ed or Edward, not Eddie.'

'I'll call you Edward, then. I had an Uncle Edward once. He had a bald head under his hat and an enormous belly.'

Edward laughed at the colourful description of Tommy's relative, pleased to have made a new friend already.

'How long have you been here?' asked Edward.

'A long time. I used to live with me Aunty Mary at Silksworth until she got too old to look after me. She died when I was nine.'

After breakfast, the children walked to church, and Edward was grateful that Tommy walked by his side. He heard several snide comments directed towards him, but Tommy soon put a stop to them. Sometimes, he told the children to shut their mouths, and sometimes, just a look from him was enough to silence them.

They spent several hours at church in the morning, went back to the orphanage for their midday meal, and then returned to the church in the afternoon. Edward had never heard so many sermons and prayers in one day before, and his head was spinning. They had some free time before and after the evening meal, which he spent with Tommy in the communal room, and when the bell rang to signal it was time for bed, they parted reluctantly.

In his bedroom, Edward looked under his pillow, in his bed and underneath it. He couldn't find the nightshirt he'd left crumpled under his pillow anywhere. He heard one of the boys tittering under his covers, and then a few more boys began to laugh, too.

'Who has me nightshirt?' asked Edward, looking at the boys.

The laughter got louder.

Edward wanted to cry, but he didn't. He went to the nearest bed and pulled down the bedclothes.

'What do you think you're doin'?' asked a fair-haired boy with a scar across his forehead. 'This is my bed!'

'Do you have it?' asked Edward.

'If you can't see it, I ain't got it.' The boy smirked.

A dark-haired boy on the other side of the room was watching, his cheeks red and his eyes glowing.

Edward reckoned that he must be the one who took the nightshirt, so he pulled the cover off his bed, and there it was, crumpled up by the boy's dirty feet. A wave of anger filled Edward, and he thumped the boy on the chin, but he was knocked to the floor before he had time to reclaim the nightshirt.

Four boys beat him, kicked him, and called him names. They pulled him up and held him firmly, and the fair-haired boy said, 'Stan, he's all yours.'

Stan, the boy that Edward had punched, got out of bed with an evil gleam in his eye. Raising his right hand, he made a fist and thumped Edward in the stomach, winding him, but Edward couldn't double over as he was still held upright by the other boys. The pain was unbearable. Then, a second blow landed on his chin, and he slipped into unconsciousness.

He opened his eyes to see Mrs Kelly standing over him.

'He's comin' round!' she shouted.

And then, Mr Kelly's face was floating above him, and the smell of alcohol made him want to move away, but he couldn't.

'Thank God, for that,' said Mr Kelly, sighing loudly. 'I thought he was done for. If we'd lost him, we'd have had to give all that money back to Lord Malham.'

Through the haze, Edward thought he'd misjudged the Kellys at first and that they did care about him, but from the conversation, it soon became apparent that it was the money they were bothered about, not him.

'Mebbe he should have a room of his own,' said Mrs Kelly. 'He'd be safer that way. There's a small one in the attic that's empty.'

'Aye, that's a good idea. We're gettin' five times more for havin' him here than any of the others can hope to make, so we'd better take good care of him. If we want to retire to the seaside, we can't afford to lose that money.'

Edward tried to sit up, but when the room started to spin, he groaned and lay back on the sofa.

'You stay there, Eddie, until you're feelin' better. Do you

hear me?' Mrs Kelly's voice got quieter, and Edward drifted back to sleep.

The next time he awoke, Mr and Mrs Kelly were sitting by the fire. Mr Kelly had a beer bottle on the table beside him, and Mrs Kelly was sewing a quilt. Edward lay still for several minutes before they noticed he was awake.

'How are you feelin', Eddie? Any better?' asked Mrs Kelly as she crossed the room and sat on the end of the sofa.

Edward nodded.

'I've made a bed for you up in the attic. If you're still a bit shaky, Mr Kelly will help you get up them stairs.'

Edward managed to stand up but grabbed the back of the sofa as the room spun around, and he feared he would fall.

'You're goin' to have to help him, Bill. He'll not make it up them stairs by himself.'

Mr Kelly carried Edward up three flights of stairs and into a small room. At first glance, Edward thought it looked cosier than the room he'd shared with the boys and that it would be nice to be away from the bullies.

As he climbed into bed, he thought it funny that he would sleep in his clothes because his nightshirt was still in Stan's bed. Edward didn't know if he laughed out loud or if it was only in his head. His head hurt, and after he'd climbed into bed, he placed his hand on his brow to ease the pain and soon fell asleep.

The next day, Mrs Kelly told Edward to stay in bed and rest, and she brought food to his room at mealtimes. By that evening, he was feeling much better, so he got out of bed and explored the room.

There was a small window, about six inches high and two feet long, between the floorboards and the slope of the roof, which let in a surprising amount of light. The walls were whitewashed. His bed was covered in a grey blanket. At the head of the bed stood a small chest with three drawers—the top one contained his clothes, and he realised he was wearing a nightshirt but couldn't remember who had removed his clothes and dressed him in it; the middle drawer contained an old dog-eared bible; and the bottom drawer was empty.

He couldn't see Dorothy's black ribbon anywhere, so he crept downstairs to his old room and was relieved to find the boys were sleeping. He opened the drawers next to his old bed, one by one, and found what he was looking for in the bottom drawer. Pleased that he'd found the ribbon, he carried it back to the attic room and placed it on his pillow, thinking about his friends at Rookhope as he drifted off to sleep.

At breakfast the following morning, Tommy asked, 'Where were you yesterday? I thought someone must have come to claim you and taken you away. I was worried that you'd gone and left me.'

Edward explained what had happened, and Tommy was livid.

'I told them to leave you alone!' he said.

Standing to his full height, Tommy charged at Stan, who almost choked on his porridge when Tommy knocked him off his chair, landed heavily on top of him, and began to punch him.

It took Mr Kelly and two of the older boys to pull Tommy away from him.

Stan lay on the floor, moaning loudly and clutching his chest.

Mrs Kelly knelt by his side and ran her hands over his chest, and Stan screamed.

31

'I think he's broken his ribs,' she said to her husband. 'You'd better take him up to bed.'

When Mr Kelly returned, his face was white and strained. His voice sounded strained, too.

'I'm surprised at you, Tommy Bell,' he said. 'Stan will be off work for a month or two 'cos of what you've done to him. That's at least a month's worth of wages that we'll not get in because of your disgraceful conduct.'

Edward saw Mr Kelly drag Tommy out of the dining room and was worried about what would happen to him because Mr Kelly looked very angry. When Tommy didn't appear for the evening meal that day, Edward feared that he might have been sent away, and that fear grew as the week went on.

He didn't see Tommy again until the following Monday when he entered the dining room for breakfast. His friend's cheeks looked hollow, and he had dark circles under his red-rimmed eyes.

'Have you been poorly?' asked Edward.

'No.'

'So, where have you been? I was worried about you.'

Tommy looked from side to side, ensuring he wouldn't be overheard.

'He locked me in the cupboard under the stairs.'

'For a whole week?' Edward's eyes were wide and his mouth open.

'Aye, if you say so. It felt like much longer to me.'

'Did they feed you?'

'He brought me a bit of bread and a tankard of water once a day and he swapped the bucket.'

'The bucket?'

'Aye, you know, for doin' your business in, like a po.'

Edward could hardly believe what he was hearing. *How could anyone be so cruel to a child?*

'The worst thing was that he never said a word to me in all that time,' said Tommy. 'He never said how long he'd keep me locked up for. It was like livin' in Hell, not knowin' if he'd ever let me out. Edward, I was scared. I thought I was goin' to die in there all alone.'

Tommy hid his face and wiped it with his sleeve.

'That's awful, Tommy,' said Edward, putting a hand on his friend's arm. 'Mr Kelly should not have done that to you. He never locked Stan in the cupboard when he knocked me out. If he had, then you wouldn't have been able to hit Stan and you wouldn't have got into trouble.'

'I'd hit him again if he hurt you, Edward, even if it meant I'd get locked in the cupboard again. I said I'd look out for you when you came here and I meant it.'

At that moment, Edward knew he had a friend for life. He could depend on Tommy Bell no matter what, and for the first time, he thought he knew what it must feel like to have a big brother.

After breakfast, Edward returned to his room and didn't know what to do. He was bored when the older children were out at work during the day. Lying on his bed, he idly wondered about running away but didn't know where he'd run to. He couldn't leave Tommy either, not now that they were firm friends. Anyway, his father knew he was at the orphanage and that knowledge made him feel safe and secure. If he ran away, he might never see his father again, ruining his father's plans for his future. So, after weighing up the pros and cons, he decided to stay at the orphanage, and he would look forward to his sixteenth birthday when he would discover where his future lay.

'There you are, Eddie!' said Mr Kelly. 'You start your lessons this mornin'. Come downstairs and meet your tutor.'

Edward followed him down the three flights of stairs to the ground floor, where he saw a young red-haired man with a neatly trimmed beard.

'This is Edward Earle,' said Mr Kelly. 'We call him Eddie. This here is Mr Peters. He's goin' to teach you lots of new things, aren't you, Mr Peters?'

'Yes, that's right.'

'I know how to read and write. I've been goin' to school since I was four and I was the best in me class at readin'.'

'I can assure you, Edward,' said Mr Peters, 'that there are still a great many things you have yet to learn. Let's go to the classroom and make a start, shall we?'

Edward was happy that Mr Peters had used his proper name and was intrigued to find out what more he could learn. He followed the teacher into the classroom without hesitation.

Chapter 6

The Orphanage, Sunderland
June 1758

On several consecutive days, Edward noticed a small girl sitting in the communal room after the other children left for work. Every time he passed the doorway, she appeared to be looking out of the window, which intrigued him.

'Good morning!' he said, moving to her side and tilting his head to see through the window. 'What are you watching?'

'The clouds,' she said dreamily. 'They're different every day and sometimes I can see shapes, like animals and boats and faces.'

Edward smiled at her and said, 'I'm Edward. What's your name?'

'Mary Jane Wright.'

He held out his hand and said, 'It's good to meet you, Miss Mary Jane Wright.'

She giggled as she shook his hand.

Edward had an idea. He spent fewer hours in the classroom than Tommy spent at work and was often lonely until Tommy returned, and Mary Jane was alone all day now that she no longer went to work. He reckoned it would make sense for them to keep each other company.

'Would you like to learn to write, Mary Jane?'

'Do you know how?' she asked, wide-eyed.

'Yes. I can teach you if you like.'

She nodded at him eagerly. 'I would love to be able to write my name.'

He showed her to the classroom, and they started their first lesson. Mary Jane held the quill awkwardly at first, but her pen strokes soon became more confident as she practised drawing simple lines and curves.

Edward introduced Mary Jane to Tommy after the evening meal that day, and they sat in the communal room together, where both Edward and Mary Jane enjoyed listening to Tommy's tales about the factory, the docks and the town. The following evening, Edward began to read the story of King Arthur to Tommy and Mary Jane, and the night after that, Tommy taught Edward and Mary Jane a folk song he'd heard at the docks. On Sunday morning, she walked to church with them, and soon the three of them were inseparable. Mary Jane was like a little sister to them; the boys enjoyed her company and grew protective of her.

Edward continued with her lessons. Mary Jane was a good student and a quick learner, and within a few weeks, she could write her name without any mistakes. Edward continued to teach her to write simple words, and the grin on her face when she completed a new word was reward enough for him.

During the course of their friendship, Edward discovered that Mary Jane was ten years old, just a year younger than himself, but she looked younger. He knew that she had worked at the pin factory and never asked her why she didn't go there anymore; it was evident from her thin frame and persistent cough that she had tuberculosis. There was a death sentence hanging over her. In the back of his mind, Edward knew that, but he never dwelt on it.

One morning, a few months after Edward had befriended Mary Jane, she struggled to walk to church. Without a word, Tommy picked her up and carried her. She tried her best to sing the hymns that day, but her chest was worsening, and she struggled to catch her breath. Edward listened to her, fearing her health was deteriorating quickly.

After the service, Tommy carried her back to the orphanage and placed her on a chair in the communal room next to the window where she liked to sit.

'When did you start to feel ill?' asked Tommy.

'When I worked at the pin factory,' she said. 'A lot of the children there had consumption. I think I must have caught it off them.'

'Don't worry. We'll look after you,' said Tommy. 'You'll soon get better.'

She smiled sweetly at him and said, 'Thank you, Tommy. You're very kind.'

Edward realised from that short interaction that Mary Jane knew she was dying but didn't tell Tommy to spare his feelings, and a lump formed in his throat.

Edward was worried about Mary Jane when she didn't come to breakfast the following day. Boys were not allowed to go into the girls' bedrooms, but he sneaked in as nobody else was around. She was lying in bed, turned her head to him, and smiled weakly. Knowing she liked to look at the sky, he pushed her bed to the window so she could see out, and he read to her until she fell asleep. Reluctantly, he left her bedside when he heard the children returning from work.

The following day, Mr Kelly stood before the children at breakfast and said, 'I have some sad news to impart. Mary Jane Wright passed away last night. Let's all pray for her soul.'

Edward felt the sting of tears in his eyes when he listened to the prayer, and he heard Tommy sniffling beside him. Poor Mary Jane. She had never experienced a mother's love, playing outside in the sun, riding a pony or swimming in a river—the things he'd enjoyed before coming to the orphanage. Her short life had been full of suffering—working long hours, disease and pain, yet she had never once complained. She was the bravest person he had known.

He was glad he'd been able to spend time with her and hoped he had helped ease her final weeks. He wondered if she might have lived longer or even survived if she'd been in a loving home surrounded by her family and not been forced to work from dawn to dusk as she had at the orphanage—until she could work no more.

Mary Jane Wright's funeral was held at the local church they attended on Sundays. Mr Kelly and Edward were the only witnesses to Reverend Scope's short and impersonal service. Tommy had wanted to be there, but Mr Kelly insisted that he went to work that morning.

Her body was buried in a pauper's grave at the far corner of the churchyard. A tear ran down Edward's cheek as they lowered the shrouded body into the ground, and he couldn't help feeling bitter that the Kellys hadn't thought her worth the price of a coffin.

Apart from Tommy and me, who will remember dear Mary Jane?

Chapter 7

The Orphanage, Sunderland
March 1760

At six o'clock, Mrs Kelly sounded a bell to wake the children, but Edward was already awake. It was his thirteenth birthday, the third birthday he'd spent at the orphanage, and he had three more to endure before he could leave the place. He couldn't wait to go—the two years and seven months he'd already been there had felt like an eternity.

Life at the orphanage would have been unbearable without Tommy and Mr Peters's lessons. He took a keen interest in all subjects and learned far more than he'd thought possible. When he wasn't in the classroom, he brought books to his attic room to study there. The Kellys allowed him the use of a candle to read by its light, and as nobody ever came to the attic to check on him, he often read late into the night.

Edward watched the business of the orphanage with a learned eye, and it didn't take him long to work out that the Kellys were making good money from it—to the detriment of the children. The house had six bedrooms, three for boys and three for girls, and about thirty children usually stayed there.

The Kellys preferred to take in older children who could work, from ten to fourteen years of age, but a couple of the older girls cared for a few babies and toddlers.

He observed that the Kellys did very little work themselves. The children made their beds and cleaned their rooms. A few girls prepared, cooked and served the meals, washed the dishes and performed all the laundry duties. Most of the children were employed outside of the orphanage, too. A few swept chimneys, but most worked at the manufactories in the town, making pins, glass and rope. When the boys were old enough, they were apprenticed to the sea service and trained aboard ships, and the girls were placed as domestic servants in and around Sunderland.

Tommy worked at the rope factory by the docks. Edward loved to hear the tales the sailors told him, but he feared that Tommy might disappear one day and sail away from Sunderland with them. At fourteen years old, he was big and strong and would make a good sailor.

The Kellys' income came from the wages of the orphans. Edward had calculated how much the children earned from their employment, estimated the costs involved in their keep and concluded that the Kellys made quite a tidy sum from running the orphanage.

As he descended the stairs for breakfast, he contemplated the ways in which the orphans' lives could be improved if only the Kellys would spend a little more on them—the children would welcome an extra blanket in winter for warmth; most of them could not read and write, and teaching them their letters and numbers could improve their prospects; slightly larger portions of food and more variety would be good too; occasionally a doctor should be consulted when the children were sick; and providing a coffin for a child who had died in their care was not too much to ask.

Meals at the orphanage were the same every day—porridge for breakfast, bread with a little dripping or cheese at noon, and broth or stew with bread or potatoes in the evening. Edward missed his mother's cooking. She'd had a small garden next to her house at Rookhope, and he remembered eating fresh vegetables, eggs and fruit. His mouth watered at the thought of her delicious apple pie.

There was so much on his mind, and now that he was thirteen, he decided that after breakfast would be a good time to talk with Mr Kelly about the orphanage business.

As usual, Edward sat next to Tommy, watched the girls carry bowls of thin porridge to the tables, and set them down in front of the children. A new boy picked up his spoon and ate hungrily, and the room fell silent.

Mr Kelly, who overlooked the proceedings every morning, shouted, 'What have we here? A little heathen who eats without sayin' grace!'

The boy put down his head in shame.

'I'll see you in my office. Now!'

The boy's chair scraped the floor as he got to his feet, which earned him a stern look from Mrs Kelly, and he stumbled past the other chairs on his way to the office.

Edward felt sorry for the boy. He'd been summoned to the office several times when he first arrived at the orphanage. It wasn't just the blows that had hurt; the words had stung too. Mr Kelly took every opportunity to remind the children of how lucky they were to be housed under his roof, cared for by Mrs Kelly, and disciplined by himself, and none more so than when he had a child bent over his knee and a wooden

41

ruler or a leather belt in his hand.

The boy returned several minutes later, his eyes red, and he sat uncomfortably on the chair.

When Edward finished eating and left the room, he put a hand on the boy's shoulder to let him know he was not alone. He walked to Mr Kelly's office, knocked at the door and entered when bidden.

'Sir, I wondered if I may have a few minutes of your time.'

'Yes, Eddie, sit down. What's troublin' you?'

'Well, to tell you the truth, you are,' he said, looking Mr Kelly directly in the eye.

'What!' said Mr Kelly, rising from his chair, 'How dare you?'

'I dare, Mr Kelly, because I know everything about this place. I know how much money is coming in and the costs of keeping the children, and I know that you're doing very well from it. I also know that you enjoy beating the children, and you should be ashamed of yourself.'

'Now, you listen here you little upstart—' shouted Mr Kelly.

'No, sir, you'll listen to me. I know you won't throw me out on the streets because you want the money that came with me. I would like to see more of the children's wages spent on the children and fewer punishments. The children work hard for you and you should respect that. Don't forget that if I'm not happy and I walk out of that door, it won't be long before Lord Malham's man would return to take back the money he gave you.'

Mr Kelly sat down, his face reddening, and put his head in his hands.

Edward left him, feeling pleased that he had spoken out in an attempt to help his fellow orphans, and went to the classroom for his lessons.

Learning came quickly to him; he could read and write as well as a scholar, and his understanding of mathematics was good, too. Mr Peters had done his duty teaching him the subjects his father had requested, but as they had three more years to fill before Edward could leave the orphanage, the tutor suggested he teach him other topics such as history, geography, the classics, Latin and French. Mr Peters did not teach religion in the classroom at Edward's request because he had more than enough of that at church.

'Good Morning, Edward, and happy birthday!' said Mr Peters.

'Thank you,' Edward replied. 'What are we studying today?'

'There has been a terrible fire at Boston, Massachusetts. Do you know where that is?'

'It's in America, sir.'

'That's right. This morning we will explore a map of America, we'll look at where the main towns are located, and then I want you to tell me why you think they were built in those places.'

Edward enjoyed these tasks. He loved to think about faraway lands and the people who lived there. He studied maps of England too, and when he'd found the tiny hamlets of Redburn, Boltsburn and Stotsfieldburn in the Rookhope Valley, he had been overjoyed, but his joy quickly subsided when he realised how many miles he was from home.

He found school days fun, Saturdays long and boring, and Sundays tediously dull. Even though he had more time with Tommy on Sundays, they spent most of the day at church. It was full of sermons and prayers from morning until night. Edward had shown interest in religion initially, but his enthusiasm soon wore off, and he reckoned he'd had enough in three years to last him a lifetime.

Reverend Scrope, with his inexpressive face, monotone voice and lifeless narrative, was the most severe man that Edward had ever met. Tommy had once said the vicar was the only man on earth not to have a funny bone in his body, and Edward had laughed so hard that he'd cried.

Even so, Sundays were to be endured, a test of patience, and more often than not, Edward let his mind wander, thinking about the things he would like to do when he eventually left the orphanage, and one thing was for sure, that would not include attending church.

Chapter 8

The Orphanage, Sunderland
March 1763

Three years later, Edward looked around the attic room for the last time. He felt no regret leaving the orphanage because it had felt like a prison rather than a home for the five years he had spent there. Tommy had left over a year earlier, and it hadn't been the same without him.

He removed Dorothy's black ribbon from his drawer and tied back his hair. He glanced at the ragged old bible and chose not to take it. A change of clothes lay on his bed. He bundled them together and carried them downstairs.

Pausing outside Mr Kelly's office, he knocked lightly at the door, and it opened.

'Ah, Eddie. I see you're ready to leave us,' said Mr Kelly.

'Yes, sir.'

'Please sit.' The man pointed at a chair.

'But I was just about to leave.'

'I know that, but there is somethin' I need to give you.'

Edward entered the room and sat in the familiar chair. It was where he had sat every time Mr Kelly had scolded him for whatever misdemeanours he had committed during his early years there. The chat he'd had with Mr Kelly three years earlier had protected him from further discipline, but unfortunately, he had failed to help the other children as much as he'd intended.

'As you know, when you came here,' said Mr Kelly, 'your benefactor left some money for your upkeep. Most of it has been spent on your education, clothing and food, but there is a small amount of it remaining.'

Mr Kelly opened a drawer in his bureau and counted some notes and coins.

Edward was surprised when the man handed him two pounds and six shillings, which seemed like a fortune to a boy who had only seen pennies and halfpennies, and those had been few and far between. He wondered why Mr Kelly had given the money to him when he could have kept it for himself; he wasn't known for his generosity.

Lord Malham's butler's words travelled back to him through the years, 'His Lordship will keep a close eye on this boy.'

Edward wondered if Mr Kelly was worried that Lord Malham would find out about the unspent money and send someone to collect it.

'Thank you, sir,' said Edward.

'I trust you will lead an honest and decent life as God intended, Eddie Earle, and as befittin' an orphan from this establishment.'

'Can I go now?' asked Edward.

Mr Kelly raised his eyebrows.

'Please may I go, sir?'

'You have the manners and the voice of a gentleman when you choose to use them, young man. They should stand you in good stead for the future. Yes, you can leave now, and may

God go with you.'

Mr Kelly held out his hand, and Edward shook it, then walked out of the office without a backward glance. He strode down the dingy hallway and opened the large wooden door, thinking about how much he hated the name Eddie. Only the Kellys and the children at the orphanage had ever called him Eddie, and he would never let anybody call him Eddie again.

Edward squinted when the full force of the morning sunlight hit his eyes. Before they had time to adjust to the light, he was lifted off the step and swung around, and he heard his friend's laughter.

'I don't believe it!' exclaimed Tommy. 'We're free of this place forever. We can do anythin' we want! Come on, I'll take you home.'

'Where are we going?' asked Edward, walking by Tommy's side.

'Me auntie left me her house in the woods near Silksworth. I'm not supposed to get it 'til I'm twenty-one, but nobody lives there so I have been. You can stay there with me.'

'Sounds good to me.'

They left the streets of Sunderland and walked for almost an hour until they reached a dense woodland and took a narrow track through the trees. It led to a small clearing where an old stone cottage with a thatched roof stood. At first glance, Edward thought it looked beautiful. A place of their own to live, just the two of them, but as he drew nearer, he could see that the roof had been patched; in fact, he thought there might be more patches than the original thatch. The small-paned windows were covered in grime and sap from the trees. The wood store outside the door was packed—at least they could have a fire and keep warm.

47

Edward waited for Tommy to unlock the door, but instead of taking a key from his coat pocket and placing it in the lock, Tommy pushed it open.

'Don't you lock it?' asked Edward.

'No need. I've got nothin' to steal. Nobody comes around here anyway.'

Looking back at their journey, Edward realised that Tommy was right. They'd not passed anyone for ages before they reached the cottage. It was more secluded than he'd imagined.

The cottage had only one room. There was a small fireplace with dried moss and sticks in the grate ready to light, a table with two chairs, one tatty armchair and two straw mattresses on the floor.

Edward's stomach rumbled loudly. 'I'm hungry,' he said. 'Have you got anything to eat?'

Tommy looked sheepish.

'Don't you have any food here?'

Edward began to panic. He wasn't used to fending for himself and feared he might starve, for there were no shops or taverns nearby that he'd seen.

'Come with me,' said Tommy. 'I know where we can get somethin'.'

The boys walked to the edge of the woods and along the road until they came to a farm.

Looking in all directions, Tommy said, 'There's nobody about. Wait here.'

Tommy climbed through a small gap under the hedgerow and ran to a wooden shed down the field. He opened the door and went inside. When he came out, he waved his hands in the air, holding something that Edward couldn't see from that distance, and then he ran back to the breach in the hedge.

Tommy reappeared on the roadside and handed Edward four white eggs.

Edward's mouth watered. He hadn't eaten an egg since he'd moved to Sunderland five years ago, but back home, his mother had regularly cooked him eggs for breakfast. He hadn't realised how much he'd missed them.

They returned to the cottage, and Tommy boiled the eggs in a pan over the fire for their tea.

Wondering how they could afford food, Edward asked, 'Have you got a job?'

'I chop wood for the forester on the estate sometimes,' replied Tommy. 'He pays me for it. But it's not regular work. He just knocks at the door when he needs help and asks me if I can give him a hand.'

Edward thought Tommy would be well-suited to forestry work, with him being a large, muscular fellow. He'd often boasted about his strength at the orphanage and had surprised the boys one day when he lifted four of them at once.

He, himself, was tall and slim and not particularly strong. While Tommy had been making ropes in Sunderland, Edward had sat in a classroom. He knew he wouldn't be any good at forestry work. He needed to find a job where he could use his learning; that's where his skills lay.

'Where's the nearest town to here?' asked Edward.

'Silksworth—it's just a small place, more of a village really, but it's just up the road, or there's Sunderland.'

'I'll go to Silksworth tomorrow and find a job.'

Tommy laughed. 'It's not that easy to find a job unless you want to work on the keelboats. They're always takin' lads on. But I can't see you as a keel man.'

Edward smiled and said, 'No, I have no intention of working

49

on the keels. I had office work in mind, or maybe teaching. I enjoyed teaching Mary Jane.'

Tommy looked impressed. 'Good luck to you!'

When Edward was sure that Tommy was asleep that night, he searched the room for somewhere to hide the money that Mr Kelly had given to him. He felt the walls for loose stones but didn't find any, and then he tread on each floorboard until one moved. A small section under the table was loose. He lifted it and tucked the money away to one side so that it wouldn't be seen if anyone removed the board. Happy that he'd found a safe place to store it, he climbed into bed and soon fell asleep.

The next morning, Edward set off for Silksworth. The narrow road followed the edge of the wood, and Edward was amazed to see a roe deer cross his path and disappear into the cover of the trees. The sound of songbirds filled his ears and lifted his spirits. Walking through the countryside reminded him of Rookhope; fleetingly, he felt homesick. He had seen few wild animals and birds in Sunderland, only stray dogs, cats, seagulls, and sparrows that he could recollect.

When he reached Silksworth, he was surprised at how small the place was, much smaller than Sunderland, and looking around, he wondered if he should have returned to the town to find work instead, but he was here now, so he decided he might as well try.

A well-dressed man walked along the road, and when he drew near, Edward said in his best voice, 'Excuse me, sir. Are there any offices or schools around here? Or do you know of anyone seeking a teacher or a clerk?'

The gentleman looked him up and down sceptically. Edward blushed slightly. He knew his clothes did not match his voice or his education. Perhaps he should have used some of his father's money to buy a decent outfit before seeking work.

'Dr Page lives in that house over there,' the man replied, pointing at a large detached house further along the road. 'There's a solicitor on the main street. A few shops. Oh! And there's the estate office on the edge of the village. That's all I can think of. There aren't any schools around here. Perhaps you should try in Sunderland—there'll be more jobs on offer there.'

As Edward wanted to stay with Tommy in his cottage in the woods, he needed to find employment as close as possible. Silksworth would be ideal if only he could find a suitable vacancy. He thanked the man, went to the doctor's surgery, and rapped on the door.

'Good morning, sir,' said Edward brightly. 'I am seeking a position and wondered if you might have any suitable work for me.'

'You're too young to be a doctor,' said the doctor, smiling kindly. 'What kind of work are you looking for exactly?'

'I'm not sure. I've been educated in arithmetic, literature, history, geography, Latin, French and the classics. I read and write very well.'

'I have no doubt of it. But I only have need of a medical man, not a scholar. Have you been to see Mr Travis?'

Edward shook his head.

'He's a solicitor and you'll find him on the high street. I believe he may be looking for a clerk.'

'Thank you, sir,' said Edward sincerely. 'Thank you very much.'

A few minutes later, Edward knocked at the solicitor's door, and a woman opened it. Edward explained his quest, and she invited him to come inside. He sat in a small room lined with chairs and suspected it was a waiting room for clients.

A middle-aged gentleman entered and shook Edward's hand while looking him up and down.

'I'm Mr Travis. My wife has told me that you arc Edward Earle and that you're seeking employment, is that right?'

'Yes, sir. That's correct.'

'Please, come into my office.'

Edward followed him into another room and sat at the table indicated by the man, who placed a quill, ink pot and parchment on the table in front of him.

'Let me see how well you write.'

'What shall I write, sir?' asked Edward.

Mr Travis took a document from his desk, a property deed, and said, 'Make a copy of this,' then he sat at his desk to continue his work.

Ten minutes later, Edward held up the parchment and said, 'I've finished, sir. Would you care to take a look at it?'

'Bring it to me.'

Studying Edward's transcript, Mr Travis read every word before raising his eyes to the young man.

'Your letter formation is more modern than mine, but it's clear and consistent despite the speed in which you completed the task. There is not a single error in the transcription. Well done, Edward. This is excellent work. Did you have difficulty with the Latin words?'

'No, sir. I recognised them all.'

'You are an enigma, Edward Earle. Where on earth did you learn Latin and to write in a hand like this?'

'At the orphanage in Sunderland, sir. Money was provided for my education there.'

'I see. That would explain it. And your poor clothing too,' said Mr Travis sadly. 'I would like you to start here on Monday morning, and I will give you an advance on your wages so you can buy a suitable outfit for work.'

'Thank you, Mr Travis.' Edward beamed at him. 'That's very kind of you.'

Before he left, Mr Travis gave him some coins. Edward wandered around the village and found a tailor's shop, where he purchased a new coat, breeches, waistcoat and two pairs of woollen socks, and a bakery, where he bought a loaf of bread.

He ran back to the woods, eager to tell Tommy his good news.

Chapter 9

White Hall Farm, Rookhope
July 1764

Edward jumped off the cart and thanked the farmer for the ride. He pulled down his hat to shield his eyes from the sun and surveyed the hillside, looking for White Hall Farm, which he had not seen for seven years.

As he ascended the hill, he thought about the days leading up to this visit. Until Friday, he'd had no intention of returning to Rookhope, not after Mr Robson had abandoned him at Granby Hall when his mother died.

It was Mr Travis who had put the idea into his head. Edward enjoyed his work in the solicitor's office and had never considered taking time off, but as Edward put on his coat to leave the office on Friday evening, Mr Travis said, 'You've worked here for well over a year, Edward, and you've not taken a single day's leave in all that time. Wouldn't you like to take a week off, go somewhere, visit someone, take a vacation?'

His question had made Edward think about where he would like to go, and the only place that sprang to mind was White Hall Farm, the Robsons' home, at Rookhope. He'd thanked Mr Travis for the suggestion and agreed to take a week's leave to visit his friends.

The trip from Silksworth to Rookhope had taken a day and a half. Edward had managed to hitch rides for most of the journey, and he'd spent the night sleeping on a grassy verge at Wolsingham, not wanting to waste money on lodgings when it was warm and dry outdoors.

As he climbed further up the hill, the scent of newly cut grass hung heavily in the air, and childhood memories came flooding back. He wondered how John and Dorothy were. John was a year older than him, so he'd be eighteen now, and Dorothy was a year younger, so she would be sixteen.

Would John be working on his father's farm, in the lead mines or at the smelt mill? Would Dorothy be helping her mother at home or working in service elsewhere?

He hoped to see them both during his visit; he'd missed them dreadfully when he left Rookhope.

Edward reached the brow of the hill, saw White Hall Farm in the distance and immediately felt a sense of belonging; it looked so familiar. People were working in the field in front of the house, turning the rows of cut grass with wooden rakes to dry it in the sun. He tried to make out the figures but couldn't from that distance. He guessed that the Robson children would have changed enormously in seven years.

John was the first to spot him walking towards the farm. He dropped his hay rake and ran towards him.

'Ed! It is you, isn't it?'

Edward felt John's strong arms wrap around his body, hugging him tightly.

When John stepped back, there were tears in his eyes, and he said, 'I can't believe you're here! I didn't think we'd see you again.'

Remembering the boy he had played with at the farm, Edward looked at the young man standing before him. His messy brown hair and hazel eyes were the same. He had grown to almost six feet tall, just a couple of inches shorter than Edward, but he was much broader around the shoulders and chest. His arms were tanned, his hands calloused, and his voice deep and friendly.

'So, you're working on the farm now?' asked Edward.

'Listen to you,' said John, chuckling. 'You sound different.'

'Yes, I suppose I must. I had elocution lessons to rid me of my northern accent. Oh, John! We have so much to catch up on.'

'That we have. To answer your question, I work here on the farm in the evenings and at weekends, and I work at the smelt mill the rest of the week, like me father does.'

Dorothy stepped out of the house and saw the two men greet each other. At first, there was no recognition in her eyes of the tall, slim figure with his long dark hair tied back in a ribbon at the base of his neck. Then, suddenly, she realised who he was and ran over to him and hugged him tightly.

'Edward,' she said. 'It's so good to see you.'

'Go on, say somethin' to our Dot,' said John. Turning to his sister, he said, 'He speaks all hoity-toity now.'

'Good afternoon, Dorothy,' said Edward, taking her hand and kissing it as he had seen gentlemen do, and he was shocked by the effect his actions had on her. He thought she might swoon.

When she recovered, she smiled at him and said, 'Come inside. I bet you're hungry, aren't you?'

All three of them went indoors, longing to renew their acquaintance and fill in the missing years.

'Edward Earle!' exclaimed Mrs Robson when he walked through the door. 'My God! It is you. You've grown into a fine-looking, young man. If only your mother could see you, she'd be so proud.'

'Let him get in and have a seat, Mother,' said Dorothy. 'I'll get him somethin' to eat.'

'Have you come all the way from Sunderland to see us?' asked John. 'That's where me father said they took you.'

'I stayed at Sunderland until I was sixteen. I live near Silksworth now. It's a small place not far from Sunderland.'

While he answered his friend's questions, he watched Dorothy flitting around the kitchen. Her hair had darkened to a beautiful strawberry blonde, her blue eyes looked large in her heart-shaped face, and her figure had become that of a woman. Her summer working dress was low cut, and when she leaned over the table to pass him some bread and cheese, he was fascinated by the cleavage between her small, firm breasts.

'Did you hear what I said?' asked John, nudging Edward's arm.

'Sorry,' replied Edward. 'I was distracted by the food. I'm so hungry, I could eat a horse.'

Edward smiled cheekily at Dorothy, and she blushed wildly, aware of the reason for his distraction.

'Talking of horses,' said John. 'We could go for a ride this afternoon. Have a look around. See what you remember.'

'I haven't sat on a horse since I left here,' said Edward, a little dubious about the suggestion.

'It'll soon come back to you,' John reassured him. 'We have a gentle old mare. She'll look after you.'

Mr Robson came in from the field and saw Edward seated

at the table.

'How do you do, Ed?'

'How do you do, Mr Robson?' replied Edward. Mr Peters had taught him that a gentleman does not answer the question but replies in a similar fashion.

'I'm well, all things considerin'; said Mr Robson. 'With me work at the smelt mill and keepin' this farm goin', I never have a minute to meself.'

Despite his words, he sat in a chair by the fireplace, leaned back with his feet resting on the hearth, and lit his clay pipe.

'You look well, I must say,' he said, looking at Edward. 'They must have taken good care of you all these years.'

Edward thought about the severe beating he'd endured in his first week at the orphanage, the times he'd been hungry and denied food, the absence of love and affection, and Mr Kelly's discipline. Mr Kelly's eyes lit up whenever a child misbehaved and was sent to his office to be disciplined. Edward couldn't understand how anyone could enjoy using a cane or leather strap on a child as Mr Kelly did.

'Well enough,' said Edward. 'I survived the ordeal.'

'What are you doin' now? Are you workin'?' asked John.

'Yes, I'm a clerk in a solicitor's office.'

Everyone in the room looked at him, impressed that he could read and write well enough to land an office job.

'Well, well, we have gone up in the world,' said Mr Robson.

After Edward had eaten and drank two cups of tea, the two young men set off on horseback to explore the Rookhope Valley. Edward quickly found his balance on the horse and realised that she would follow John's horse with only a little prompting.

On the way out, they stopped at the small stone cottage

where Edward had lived with his mother. It was just as he remembered it; apart from it was deserted now.

'Nobody's lived in it since you left,' said John, answering his unasked question. 'Do you want to have a look inside?'

Edward slid down the horse's side, hesitantly unlatched the door, and pushed it open. It was dark inside; the small windows didn't let in much light, and dust motes filled the air. Both rooms smelled of dampness and mould. Cobwebs hung from the roof and framed the windows. The beds had been stripped of their linen, being too valuable to leave there to rot, but an iron kettle covered in dust still stood on the hearth.

Repressed memories of his mother and their brief time together in this cottage flooded his mind. He heard her voice singing to him as she had done each night and their laughter as she swung him around. He smelled lavender, her favourite flower. He remembered her drying the blooms, wrapping them in cloth, and hanging the small bundles from the rafters to make the cottage smell like summer all year round. He had loved his mother so much; she was the only family he'd ever had. Overcome with emotion, Edward's voice faltered as he said, 'Let's go.'

For the next few days, Edward got to know John and Dorothy again. He enjoyed John's company, and they grew close, becoming firm friends; it felt like they'd never been apart.

Whenever he saw Dorothy, his heart beat faster, and his hands became clammy. Sometimes, he stumbled over his words in her presence. She tended to blush when they were in each other's company, and her pink cheeks only made her look more attractive—and he was attracted to her. He couldn't get her out of his mind when he was alone in the barn at night, and even when he slept, she filled his dreams. He dreaded leaving the farm at the end of his stay because it might be months or even years before he would see her again.

The next time the young men went out riding, Dorothy joined them. Edward loved listening to her voice and hearing the sound of her laughter. He watched the movements of her body, her buttocks rising and lowering rhythmically on the saddle, her breasts straining against her dress and her loose hair flowing behind her. How he longed to touch her, smell her and kiss her.

Finally, the day he had been dreading arrived, and it was time for him to leave the farm. He said farewell to Mr and Mrs Robson and thanked them for their hospitality, which made the couple laugh as he'd slept in their barn.

He spoke to each of the children except for Dorothy. He didn't know what to say to her. When he went out into the yard, she followed him and said, 'Edward! You can't go without sayin' goodbye.'

She reached out to embrace him, and he put his arms around her and tenderly kissed her soft cheek. She stood on tiptoes and reached up to kiss his lips.

'Goodbye, Edward. I hope you'll come back soon.'

'Goodbye, Dorothy.'

Dorothy ran into the house smiling, leaving Edward feeling very alone.

John led two horses into the yard, and they rode down to Stanhope together, where John thought Edward could get a ride down the dale or maybe as far as Durham if he were lucky.

They dismounted in the marketplace, and John hugged his friend. 'I hope we don't have to wait as long to see you again,' he said sincerely.

Edward nodded, too upset to speak. He pushed John playfully on the shoulder. He wished he could have stayed longer, but couldn't because he had to return to the office on Monday.

On the journey back to Silksworth, Edward reflected on his visit to the farm. White Hall Farm was the closest thing he had to a home, and the Robsons were the closest thing he had to family, but his feelings towards Dorothy were undoubtedly not the feelings that a brother should have for a sister. Day and night, she tormented his mind and his body. He knew he would return to White Hall Farm to see her again.

Chapter 10

Granby Hall, Durham
March 1765

On Edward's eighteenth birthday, he had only one thing on his mind, something he considered well overdue, and that was seeing his father again.

It had been two years since he'd left the orphanage, and he'd waited patiently for his father to contact him, but no word had come.

Two years of waiting was long enough. Whatever his father's plans were for him, Edward was keen to find out and was confident that his education would have prepared him well. He had been told that he had a pleasant manner and a good speaking voice, and he was sure the clerk's job would serve as a good grounding for the next phase of his life, whatever it should entail.

Edward had saved enough money to buy an outfit suitable for a gentleman, and he looked the part in it.

Now, he would take matters into his own hands and visit his father.

He set off at dawn to walk the eight miles to Granby Hall. He stood outside the large wrought iron gates he remembered so vividly—the gates that he and Mr Robson had walked through to meet his father, the gates that Mr Robson had marched through when he'd abandoned him, and the gates that he'd been driven through in the ornate carriage pulled by four fine horses on the way to the orphanage.

Edward tentatively stepped through them, wondering how he would be received at the house.

Will my father be at home? Will he agree to see me? Will I finally discover what his intentions are for me?

Quickening his pace, he strode up the drive towards the mansion and knocked at the large front door.

The butler, Reynolds, opened it, and his eyes widened in recognition of the young man standing on the doorstep, now at least eighteen inches taller than the last time they had met.

'What are you doing here?' he asked.

'I've come to visit my father,' replied Edward. 'Is he at home?'

'I'm not sure he'll want to see you and to tell you the truth, I'm surprised that you want anything to do with him after he sent you to that vile place in Sunderland.'

Edward frowned. 'When you left me, you said Lord Malham would be keeping a close eye on me. I remember that very clearly.'

The butler appeared shocked that Edward had remembered his words.

'I'm afraid there's been a misunderstanding,' he said. 'I only said that so that weasel of a man wouldn't spend the money on drink. It was merely a threat, but it must have worked. I can see that the money was spent on your education as I instructed.' Looking him up and down, he said, 'You look and sound quite the gentleman.'

'Thank you,' replied Edward. 'Wasn't that the plan?'

'Plan? There was no plan. The master wanted you out of the way. Somewhere you couldn't make trouble for him.'

Edward was gutted but maintained his calm persona.

'Nevertheless,' he said, 'I should like to speak with Lord Malham.'

'As you wish,' said the butler. 'Please step inside and I'll let him know you're here.'

Edward stood in the grand hallway with its white marble columns and a wide central staircase that led to the upper storey. The house was extravagantly furnished and decorated, and the floral displays smelled wonderful. Yet, Edward hardly noticed, for he was drawn to the oil paintings that filled one wall—portraits of men and women wearing costumes from different eras.

The final picture was of the man he had met all those years ago—his father. The men in the paintings all had one thing in common—their striking green eyes. The same eyes that Edward could see reflected in the gilt mirror that hung alongside them. His portrait would have fitted in perfectly.

Edward turned when he heard footsteps approaching, expecting to see Reynolds returning to tell him that Lord Malham was indisposed, but instead, he was shocked to see Lord Malham.

Lord Malham stopped and looked at Edward, an expression on his face that Edward couldn't decipher. The two men were the same height and build, tall and slim, and looked into each other's green eyes. They also had the same dark hair, but the Lord's was thinning and speckled with grey.

'My God!' said his father. 'If there was doubt before, there is none now. Looking at you is like looking into a magic mirror where one can see one's younger self.'

'My mother was a good woman and she would not have lied about such an important matter.'

'Yes, I remember you saying that to me when you were an ill-mannered wretch. I see that you have been brought up well since then.'

Edward took his words as a slight against his mother but didn't react. He didn't want to offend Lord Malham at this early stage in their relationship. His father could see with his own eyes that he was his son, and he had admitted as much. He'd paid for his education at the orphanage, too. Surely, Reynolds had been wrong; his father must have a plan for his future.

Edward waited for his father to speak until the silence became unbearable. He wiped his sweaty palms on his breeches. If his father would not say it, then he must.

'Sir, I have come here today to find out what you have in mind for my future.'

Lord Malham looked at him quizzically, and then he laughed, the sound reverberating around the vast hallway. 'Your future,' he said, wiping tears from his eyes. 'Your future is what you will make of it, young man.'

'But—'

'I can see that you're my son by breeding, but you are not my son by law. Therefore, now that you are independent, you can expect no more assistance from me. I wish you well, Edward Earle, and I bid you good day.'

Reynolds appeared out of nowhere and ushered Edward to the front door. When they were outside, the butler said, 'I'm sorry, Edward. I know that's not what you wanted to hear, but at least he granted you an audience. That's more than most of them get.'

'You mean I'm not the only bastard he's sired?' Edward asked coldly.

'No, you're not. You must have a dozen half-brothers and sisters hereabouts. None of them are acknowledged by the family, of course, so don't take it to heart.'

'You know what?' Edward's face turned red. 'He's a disgrace. A lord should set an example, not act like a rutting tup. I wish he'd never met my mother, and I wish he wasn't my father. I want nothing more to do with that man or others like him. I hate him!'

The butler was left speechless by Edward's outpouring of emotion and hatred, but he watched with pride as Edward strode up the road.

As Edward walked home, he decided he would never think of Lord Malham as his father again, not now that he had rejected him for a second time. The first time, he hadn't been sure that his father didn't want him in his life, but this time, he was left with no doubt whatsoever.

Lord Malham could go to hell as far as he was concerned. He was an evil man and deserved nothing less, fathering illegitimate children to different mothers and living an extravagant lifestyle when so many people living better lives than him struggled to feed their families. It was so unfair.

Edward couldn't deny that he would like to live in a beautiful house that had been in the family for generations, like Lord Malham, and have money to spare. Still, if he were ever lucky enough to be in that situation, he would behave in a dignified manner and spend his money much more wisely.

He deliberated over what he would do with his money if he were rich. He'd certainly have a horse and maybe a carriage so he wouldn't have to walk everywhere. His feet were aching as he'd already walked over fourteen miles that day. He'd have nice clothes too, not lavish clothes like Lord Malham's that were merely for ornament, but well-cut clothes made from quality materials that would look smart and be serviceable. And finally, he would help people less fortunate than himself as much as he possibly could.

The most unfortunate people he'd encountered in his eighteen years of life were the children at the orphanage. He'd been far luckier than most because Lord Malham's patronage meant he had been educated rather than sent to work. The other children had a much tougher time there, working from a young age and returning so exhausted in the evenings that they often fell asleep during their meals. Mary Jane came to mind. Poor Mary Jane.

If he had a lot of money, Edward determined he would help orphans—children with nobody left in the world who cared about them. All he needed was the money to be able to do so.

His job as a clerk provided a small income, enough to feed and clothe Tommy and himself, but there was little left over at the end of the week, just a few pennies. Somehow, he had to find a way to make more money.

Edward smiled to himself. He didn't need Lord Malham's help to plan his future. He had decided what he wanted to do with his life—from now on, he would endeavour to make enough money to help the orphans in Sunderland. He felt exhilarated to have sketched out his own plan—he would fill in the details later.

When Edward returned to Silksworth Woods, he was physically exhausted from the walk. He saw Tommy chopping firewood in the clearing.

Tommy looked up, put down the axe and asked, 'How did it

go?'

'Not well,' said Edward, but there was a faint trace of a smile on his lips.

'You'd better tell me what's goin' on.'

They went inside, and Edward filled a pewter tankard from a bucket of water Tommy had drawn from the well, and he drank it all. Then, he told Tommy what had happened at Granby Hall when he'd met with Lord Malham and that afterwards, on his way home, he had resolved to be rich enough to help orphaned children.

'Have you been drinkin'?' asked Tommy.

'No, I'm deadly serious.'

Tommy paced up and down as he thought over his friend's idea.

'You know somethin',' said Tommy, 'You were lucky to get the help you got at the orphanage. I had to work from bein' a bairn, small enough to climb chimneys. And I never saw a penny of what I earned. I cannot read and write like you. I never got the chance to learn stuff like that.'

'I know,' said Edward, 'it's children like you that I want to support. If the orphanage had more money coming in from another source, like from me, they wouldn't have to send the younger children out to work, would they?'

'But how are you goin' to get rich enough to do somethin' like that?' asked Tommy. 'It would take a lot of money to replace the bairn's wages.'

Edward shrugged and said, 'I don't know.'

All of a sudden, he felt weary. How he could secure the money he would need was a problem for another day. He climbed into his bed and fell into a fitful sleep.

Images of Lord Malham filled his dreams; his laughter

echoed around his head. His father laughed at him, taunted him and humiliated him. Several times that night, Edward woke covered in sweat, his heart racing, his hands shaking, and he was more angry and vengeful each time.

He dreamt that he stole the portraits from Granby Hall, one by one, and destroyed them, removing all traces of Lord Malham's lineage, as Lord Malham had done to him by refusing to acknowledge their kinship.

Edward saw himself living a life of luxury at Granby Hall and then living as he was now, sharing a humble dwelling with a friend, with nothing of his own apart from the clothes on his back, a few pennies he had saved, and the money that Mr Kelly had given him when he'd left the orphanage, which remained untouched under the loose floorboard.

Just before he woke, Edward saw himself grow from a poor little orphan into a wealthy man. *Is that my destiny?*

Tommy had made porridge for breakfast, and they sat at the table to eat it.

'I was thinkin' about what you said last night,' said Tommy. 'If you're serious about helpin' orphans, there's only one way you could get enough money to do it.'

'How?' asked Edward, intrigued that Tommy had found a solution before he had.

'From thievin'.'

Edward remained silent, pondering the suggestion.

Tommy continued, 'When I was cleanin' chimneys, I went to a lot of the big houses in Sunderland. Some of them are full of stuff that would fetch good money, you know, cupboards and shelves full of silver. I bet there's a lot of jewellery upstairs because the women wore a lot of necklaces and stuff, and they must keep cash in the houses an' all 'cos they always paid with coins.'

Edward was deep in thought. Housebreaking was not a bad idea. Yes, it was a felony, but he'd only take from wealthy people, like Lord Malham, who could afford it and use the money he raised to help the poor. *Where was the crime in that?*

He reasoned that if only the rich people would help the poor themselves, he wouldn't need to do what he intended, but they didn't. They closed their eyes to the suffering around them and ignored the plight of the poor.

'I think that's a damned good idea,' said Edward.

Tommy grinned.

'For it to work though, we'll need to have a plan,' said Edward seriously. 'We'll need to think carefully about it before we begin.'

That evening, Edward and Tommy sat in the cottage and discussed what they would do.

'Firstly,' said Edward, 'we only ever take from those who can afford it.'

'Agreed,' said Tommy. 'And we shouldn't steal from the same house twice.'

Edward nodded and said, 'We should only take items that are easy to carry and to sell on—silver, jewellery, and money. And we'll need several shops to sell to so the shopkeepers don't become suspicious.'

'I would never have thought of that,' said Tommy.

'That's why we're together, Tommy. We've always been better when we're together, haven't we?'

Tommy nodded and smiled.

'We know how we'll raise the money,' said Edward. 'So, how do we get it to the orphans?'

'We could leave it outside the orphanage—on the doorstep.'

Edward pursed his lips. 'We could, but it might be taken by a passerby or the Kellys might keep it for themselves. There must be a record of it so that it's used correctly, but one that can't be connected to us.'

'You could pass as a gentleman,' said Tommy. 'You have the right garb and the right voice. You could go there as a bene—bene—'

'Benefactor,' finished Edward. 'Don't you think Mr Kelly would recognise me?'

'I dunno. It's got to be worth a go though.'

Edward wasn't so sure, but he nodded. 'And lastly,' he said, 'we must never, ever get caught.'

'That goes without sayin',' said Tommy sadly. 'I couldn't bear to be locked up again.'

Chapter 11

Durham Gaol
October 1770

Tommy stirred in his sleep. Edward put a hand on his friend's arm and wondered how Tommy could sleep when there was so much noise in the gaol. Day or night, it never seemed to stop—people shouting, crying, moaning and coughing.

Edward put down his head again and tried to sleep. A prisoner coughed violently and gasped for breath between more severe bouts of coughing. When the noises stopped an hour or so later, Edward knew the man had died. Death was commonplace in the gaol, but Edward wasn't surprised, considering the filth, the stench, the vermin, and the inadequate diet.

He wondered how many prisoners didn't live long enough to face trial and punishment. *Will Tommy and I survive?*

The men passed the time playing cards, yet the day still felt endless, and Tommy grew increasingly restless in his captivity.

A guard stopped outside their cell door that afternoon and sneered at them. 'Edward Earle. You're famous now, or should that be infamous?' He laughed loudly.

Edward didn't comment, and the guard looked annoyed that

he couldn't rile the prisoner.

'Your name's in the paper today, Eddie. Everyone will see you for the scoundrel that you are. They'll come in their droves to identify you as that highwayman, you can be sure of that, and then I'll watch as you fight for your life at the end of a rope.'

Tommy launched towards the guard, who stepped back even though he was behind the iron bars.

'I see your monkey has to defend you,' the guard goaded.

Edward stood up to his full height and looked down at the man. 'The only monkey around here is you,' he said coldly, 'and if you don't move away from this door right now, you'll be at the top of our visiting list when we get out of here.'

The guard looked uncomfortable as Edward stared at him. He moved away and said, 'When you get out of here. Huh! The only places you're goin' to are the courthouse and the scaffold!'

When he'd gone, Edward and Tommy sat down again, and Edward wondered who might have read the newspaper article about his arrest and what they must think of him. He was thankful that nobody had yet come forward to identify them.

What will happen if somebody identifies Tommy and me as highwaymen?

He knew the answer to that question, but it didn't bear thinking about.

Chapter 12

Sunderland Town
February 1766

Edward walked along a busy street in Sunderland, looking
for a cobbler to fix Tommy's shoes, when he saw two young
girls standing in a shop doorway, talking to people passing
by, their hands outstretched. The shopkeeper came out and
shooed them from his door, and they moved a little further
along the road and chose another spot from which to beg.

A portly gentleman walked towards them, and the girls
stepped out in front of him, stopping him sharply.

'What do you think you're doing?' he said.

'We're hungry, sir,' said the older child. 'Please spare us
somethin' so we can eat?'

'Certainly not! Get out of my way!'

The man pushed the girls forcefully, and they fell to the
ground. Then, he continued up the street, ignoring their pleas
for help.

The elder girl had grazed her knee, blood trickled down her
shin, and the younger one was holding her elbow and crying.

Edward went to them and helped them up. They were skin
and bone and had little strength.

'Stay here, I'll get you something to eat.'

Edward went to the bakery, bought two meat pies and handed them to the girls, who ate them hungrily.

'I'm Edward,' he said warmly.

'I'm Kitty, and this is my sister, Anne,' said the elder, licking gravy off her fingers.

'How old are you?' asked Edward.

'I'm seven and Anne is four.'

'And where are your mother and father?'

'They got the fever and died,' said Kitty matter-of-factly. 'On the day they were buried, a man came and chucked us out of our house, and the day after that our Elizabeth died.'

'Was Elizabeth your sister?'

'Yes, she was just a baby. We tried our best to feed her but she wouldn't drink the milk from Mr Thompson's goat. We didn't know what to do so we left her dead body on the doctor's doorstep and came to the town hopin' to get some work or somethin'.'

Their story brought tears to Edward's eyes, and he wondered why they hadn't thought to ask the doctor for help if they trusted him to bury their sister. He swallowed before saying, 'I'm sorry to hear that. When did this happen?'

'Just after Christmas.'

Edward was appalled. He couldn't believe that three young children had been left to fend for themselves and that in almost two months, not one person had come to their rescue. Without a second thought, he said, 'I know a safe place where you can stay and get some food. Would you like me to take you there?'

'Yes, please, mister.'

The girls walked with him to the orphanage he had detested

as a child. Still, at that time, if he'd had the choice of begging and sleeping rough throughout the winter months or staying at the orphanage and getting three meals a day, he would have chosen the orphanage, even if it had meant working for his keep. At least the girls wouldn't freeze to death or starve there.

He knocked at the door and stood back. A young woman he didn't recognise opened it.

'Good morning,' he said. 'I found these girls begging on the street. They've lost their parents and have nowhere to stay. Do you have room for them?'

'I'll find room for them,' she replied. 'Come in girls and we'll get you cleaned up and find you some food.'

Looking at Edward, she said, 'Thank you for takin' the time to bring them here.'

'May I ask, do Mr and Mrs Kelly still run this place?'

'No, they retired last year. They went to live in South Shields. Mr Dunsmore is the new owner.'

'Thank you. I hope the girls will be well looked after.'

'I can assure you they will be. Come on girls, follow me.'

'Thank you, mister,' said Kitty before the door closed.

Edward smiled widely as he walked away. If Mr Kelly was no longer there, he could visit the orphanage as a benefactor without being recognised.

As Edward resumed his search for a cobbler, his mind was focused on the evil man who had not only refused the girls' request for food but had pushed them out of his way as if they were diseased dogs.

He found a cobbler's shop on a side street and waited while the man nailed new soles onto Tommy's shoes. He paid for the repair and left the shop.

On his way back through the town, Edward spotted the

evil man in the crowd and decided to follow him, keeping a reasonable distance between them until they reached the edge of town. Edward watched the man open a gate, walk up the path and disappear into a large detached house at the end of the row.

Edward went to the house next door and knocked on the door. When a servant girl answered, he said, 'Excuse me. I'm sorry to bother you, but I'm looking for a friend of my father's. I believe he lives in that house there.' Edward pointed to the end house. 'Unfortunately, there's nobody at home. I just wondered if you know if Mr Wilkins still lives there.'

'No, I'm afraid not. Mr Martin lives there now. He was a ship's officer. It's a big house just for him, but he has no family that anyone knows of and he hasn't any staff either. He's too mean to pay for help, so I've been told.'

'Thank you, miss. You've been most helpful.'

The young woman smiled at him and said, 'Sorry, I don't know what happened to Mr Wilkins. I hope you find him.'

'Thank you.' Edward nodded and left, grateful that he'd found out much more than he'd expected about Mr Martin, and he was eager to tell Tommy that he'd found a potential target for their first theft.

Edward and Tommy had spent the long winter evenings discussing the intricacies of house-breaking, planning what kind of buildings they would steal from, and how they would convert their ill-gotten gains into hard cash. After months of planning, they had yet to build up the courage to commit their first crime. This was the breakthrough that they needed.

At the cottage, Edward told Tommy about the cruel behaviour he had witnessed and what he had discovered about the culprit. By the time he'd finished his tale, Tommy was angry and keen to teach the man a lesson.

'Should we go tonight?' asked Tommy.

'Why not!' said Edward. 'The sooner the better.'

The young men left the cottage at dusk, and it was completely dark when they reached the outskirts of Sunderland. The night was cloudy with no moonlight, so they were unlikely to be seen.

The house on the edge of town had a road to the front and a garden to the rear with open land behind. If they were disturbed, they could flee in that direction and then turn towards home once they were out of sight so any witnesses wouldn't see them run in the direction of Silksworth. They considered it an easy target for their first attempt, and they had no qualms whatsoever about stealing from such an obnoxious man.

When they arrived outside the house, nobody was in sight. They hid behind some hawthorn bushes at the side of the road until the light was extinguished in the upstairs room. That meant Mr Martin was in bed. They waited about half an hour, long enough for him to fall asleep, then crossed the road, went around the back of the house, and opened the kitchen window, the furthest away from where the man slept so he would be unlikely to hear them.

Edward was leaner than Tommy, so he slipped through the window, searched the house for valuables that were small enough to carry, and passed them through the window to his friend.

In the kitchen, he saw a silver teapot and a set of silver spoons. Knowing they could carry much more, he searched the downstairs rooms but saw nothing of interest. He climbed the stairs and looked in the bedrooms, avoiding the one where

Mr Martin slept. Edward found a necklace lying on a dressing table and put it in his pocket, unsure if it was made with precious stones or glass, and he picked up a silver vanity set. As he descended the staircase, one of the steps creaked loudly under his weight, and he jumped down the rest, ran through the kitchen and leapt out the window as quickly as he could.

'Quick, run!' he said to Tommy.

With the teapot in his hands and spoons rattling in his pockets, Tommy ran after Edward across the open land out of the back of the house. When they reached the trees, Edward reckoned they were safe.

They walked back through the woods, triumphant that they had done what they'd set out to do. They had their first batch of goods to sell, the proceeds of which would go to the orphans of Sunderland.

Chapter 13

Hawthorn Cottage, Sunderland
May 1766

Edward removed the stolen items from where he'd hidden them, under the old dusty hay in the stable behind the cottage, and took them into the house. He bundled them together in a thick woollen cloth.

'Are you takin' them into town today?' asked Tommy, looking up from the mat he was making.

'Yes,' replied Edward. 'Wish me luck!'

'You don't need any luck. You'll do just fine. Who's going to doubt the stuff is yours when you're dressed like that?'

Edward straightened the jacket that he'd worn to visit his father and said, 'Do I look alright?'

'Edward, you look like a gentleman. Just remember to act like one!'

Edward laughed. He set off for Sunderland carrying the bundle over his shoulder, keeping Tommy's words in mind. He must act like a gentleman to accomplish this.

Edward entered a jeweller's shop and addressed the older man behind the counter in a voice remarkably like his father's.

'Good morning! I have several items that I wish to sell.

Might you be interested in purchasing them?'

'Aye, maybe, let's take a look, shall we?'

Edward untied the cloth bag and set out the items before the jeweller—a silver teapot, a few silver spoons, a necklace and a silver vanity set.

The shop owner picked up each piece and replaced it on the counter.

'If you don't mind me sayin', this is an odd assortment you have here. If I didn't know better, I'd think you'd stolen these on your way over here.'

Edward stepped back and said, 'I beg your pardon. Are you calling me a thief?'

The man looked intently into Edward's eyes.

'What are you willing to offer me for them?' asked Edward calmly, aware that his character was being judged.

'I'm sorry, sir,' said the man stiffly. 'I can't take these. There's a pawn shop further down the street you could try.'

Edward packed the items up and left the shop, annoyed that the jeweller knew that he'd stolen the items. He was so wrapped up in his thoughts that he didn't notice a man in a dark coat watching him from the opposite side of the street or that the same man followed him down the road to the pawn shop and stood outside the grimy window watching him.

A voluptuous woman dusted the shelves inside the pawn shop, singing to herself as she worked.

'Excuse me,' said Edward, 'I have a few items here and wondered what you could offer me for them.'

'Good mornin'!' she said brightly. 'Just a minute, I'll get Harry for you.'

A few moments later, a heavily built man walked into the room. Edward thought he wasn't the sort of fellow you'd want to upset.

'What do you want?' he asked in a gruff voice.

'Would you take a look at these, please, and tell me if they might be worth something?'

Edward unwrapped the items, and the man's eyes lit up.

The man in the dark coat entered the shop and lurked in the background, pretending to be a customer queuing for service.

'Well, silver's always worth somethin'. The necklace is glass. Not worth more than a penny or so. How about I give you fifteen shillings for the lot?'

'Fifteen shillings!' said the man who stood behind Edward. 'You've been done if you accept that.'

'What's it got to do with you, Mr Bennett?' asked the pawnbroker.

'I can't stand by and watch an innocent man bein' robbed, can I?'

'Innocent man, my ass. This stuff is stolen.'

Edward stuffed the spoons and necklace in his pockets, wrapped the other items in the cloth to hide them, and left the shop without another word.

Everyone, it seemed, knew that he'd stolen them, and for the first time, he doubted that his plan would work. If he couldn't sell what he and Tommy had stolen, he'd never be able to raise money to help the orphans.

Outside on the street, Edward walked briskly until a man grabbed him by the arm.

'Stop!' said the man. 'I think we might be able to help each other out.'

Edward was interested to hear what the man in the dark coat had to say and followed him into a narrow cut between the buildings.

'Johnny Bennett's me name, and I'm pleased to meet you.' Putting his finger to his lips, he said, 'I don't need to know your name. If I'm right, and I usually am, I think you were tryin' to cash in some stolen goods back there. Well, that's what I specialise in. I'll give you a pound for that little lot.'

'It's nice to meet you, Mr Bennett.' Edward didn't know what else to say. The man was obviously a crook, but he had offered to give him money for the stolen items, which was precisely what he needed. 'Thank you, that's very kind of you.'

He knelt down, took the spoons and necklace out of his pockets, bundled them with the teapot and vanity set, and handed the package to Mr Bennett.

Johnny gave him a one-pound note, and Edward thanked him.

'You have a good eye, lad. The necklace isn't glass—it's aquamarine. It's worth shillings, not pence. The next time you've got something to sell, you come and see me or me brother, Will.' He pointed down the narrow alley and said, 'Up them steps. Knock at the door and say that Johnny sent you, and they'll let you in.'

'Thank you, Mr Bennett.'

Edward touched his hat and walked away quickly, eager to distance himself from the shady character he'd just done a deal with—but this was all part of his plan, he reminded himself. He had to convert the stolen goods into cash somehow before he could give the money to the orphanage. He didn't doubt he'd be visiting that upstairs room before long, and he was pleased that he had found somebody to buy their illicit gains from them—or that somebody had found him.

A little further up the road, he heard footsteps behind him and turned around to see if he was being followed.

'Stop, please,' a small man said, jogging to catch up with him. Edward stood and waited for the man to reach him.

'It's none of my business,' said the stranger, breathing heavily, 'but did I see you talkin' to Johnny Bennett back there?'

Edward hesitated, wondering if he should deny it, but there seemed little point when the man had clearly seen them together.

'Yes. What of it?'

'Just a word of warnin', sir. Do business with them Bennetts if you must, but never trust them. Me mate did business with them, and he disappeared about a year back. I reckon they killed him and hid his body.'

'Perhaps your friend moved away,' suggested Edward.

'Not a chance! He was a family man with a bonny wife and three little bairns. He would never have left them of his own choice.'

'Thank you for the warning. I'll keep up my guard.' He inclined his head to the man and continued on his way home.

Whether he could trust the Bennett brothers or not, he needed them. After his experience at the jeweller's shop, it was evident that he couldn't sell to various shops as he'd originally planned, so he needed somebody to fence the stolen items for him. His plan to help the orphans could not come to fruition without them.

Chapter 14

After the first burglary had gone well and they had managed to convert the stolen goods into cash, Edward and Tommy were keen to try again. This time, they chose an old manor house on the road to Seaham, whose owners spent extravagantly and entertained large numbers of guests lavishly but were cruel to their servants. They knew this because a boy from the orphanage had been placed in the stables there, and he'd returned a week later covered in bruises, claiming he'd been beaten by several men in the family.

Edward detested men who suffered from the same affliction as Mr Kelly and delighted in beating young people who couldn't retaliate.

Edward and Tommy stood outside the house until the last light was extinguished and waited until they thought the occupants would be asleep.

It was a much larger household than the first house they'd stolen from. Inside, Edward expected there would be the couple who owned it, their two teenage children, and at least four house servants. The stable hands slept above the stable, and the gardeners had cottages at the edge of the grounds.

Edward and Tommy approached the pantry window and levered it up so Edward could climb through. There was nothing in the pantry besides food, so he ventured into the kitchen, where he saw nothing of interest. He needed to find where the silverware was kept.

He crept out of the kitchen and looked into several nearby rooms, and in the third, he found what he was looking for. His eyes widened at the sight. There were shelves on all four walls, full of gleaming silver. The window was small, and some of the larger items wouldn't fit through it, yet he decided to tell Tommy to open that one, thinking it would be safer to pass the silver through it rather than carry it through the passageway to the pantry.

Edward returned to the silver room, and Tommy opened the window. Edward hurriedly passed some of the smaller items out to him, and when they had as much as they could carry, Edward looked at the window, judging it too small for him to climb out. He would have to return to the pantry to exit the house.

He walked back through the passageway, glancing into more of the downstairs rooms out of interest rather than to find more items to steal. When he reached the drawing room, he heard a floorboard creak upstairs. Someone had woken up and was moving around in the bedroom. Edward was glued to the spot.

Should I creep to the pantry window? Or should I run?

He sprinted to the pantry and bolted out of the window. Picking up the items Tommy had left for him, he said, 'Run, Tommy, run!'

The two men ran out of the grounds, and as they reached

the road, they heard the unmistakable sound of a gunshot. They froze on the spot and turned to look back at the manor house.

A plump, middle-aged man stood in the garden reloading a shotgun and lifted it to aim at them.

'Run!' shouted Edward.

They sprinted into the trees on the far side of the road and continued running until they were miles from the property. Tommy grabbed Edward's arm, and they fell to the ground, breathing heavily.

'By, that was close!' said Tommy. 'We never reckoned on him havin' a gun.'

'I didn't see it downstairs,' said Edward. 'He must sleep with it by his bed.'

'Aye, I can see why he might do that. You never know who's about.'

Edward couldn't help but laugh.

'Shush,' said Tommy. 'He might be on his way over here. We should get goin'.'

As they walked home, Edward contemplated what had just happened. They had successfully stolen a large batch of silver but could have been shot in the process. Before that night, he had never considered that their victims might have firearms in their houses, and he felt a failure for having overlooked that possibility. He vowed to be more careful in the future; he didn't want to risk his or Tommy's life to achieve his goal.

Chapter 15

Edward sat at his office desk in the late afternoon, copying a property conveyance document by candlelight, and he was struggling to keep his eyes open. Working as a clerk by day and a thief by night was taking its toll.

'Are you alright, Edward?' asked Mr Travis.

'Yes, sir. Why do you ask?'

'You look drawn. I wondered if you were coming down with some ailment or another. It's that time of year.'

'I don't think so. I feel a little tired, that's all.'

'It's a while since you had some time off work. Maybe you need a break. Take tomorrow and Friday off and come back on Monday if you feel well.'

'Thank you, sir. I'll finish this before I go.'

When Edward had completed the document, he bade farewell to his boss, put on his coat and hat, and left the office. He walked in darkness along the streets and country lanes, thinking about his dual life.

He spent the vast majority of his time working, preparing or thieving and had little time to spare. He and Tommy usually burgled one property each week, choosing a random night of the week so the police wouldn't see a pattern. The one night out stealing per week was not the problem so much as the nights he spent planning in advance; he had been very cautious since the manor house owner had taken a shot at them.

Johnny Bennett had been as good as his word and had converted their silverware into cash, and the stash of money hidden under the floorboard had grown considerably. Edward was anxious to give most of it to the orphanage, keeping only the money from Mr Kelly for himself in case he or Tommy should ever need it.

To enter the orphanage as a benefactor, he would need another set of gentleman's clothes because the outfit he'd bought to visit his father was now short in the sleeve and leg. He would also need a good background story and a lot of confidence for his deception to succeed.

Mr Travis had kindly given him a few days off work, and he decided to put them to good use. He would order suitable clothing in Sunderland so the outfit would be ready before Christmas, and he would prepare for the visit to the orphanage. He was excited to finally hand over the money he and Tommy had worked so hard to procure.

The ground sparkled with frost that evening when the moonlight hit the ground. He lifted his hands to his mouth, blew on them to warm them, and rubbed them together. He thought if there were a frost this early, it would be a cold night.

When he returned to the cottage, Edward smiled. The room was warm, with a wood fire burning in the grate, and the smell of broth made his mouth water.

'I hope you're hungry,' said Tommy, removing the pot lid

and stirring the food. 'I've made a full pan.'

'Thank you,' said Edward, taking off his coat and hat. 'That's just what I need.'

'Are we still on for tonight?' asked Tommy, ladling steaming broth into two bowls.

'Yes. You know I don't like changing plans once they're set.'

'I had a visitor today,' said Tommy, 'and it unsettled me a bit.'

Edward sat at the table and stirred the broth in his bowl, wondering who the visitor could have been when nobody knew they lived there.

'It was a messenger from your solicitor's office that came. He gave me this.' Tommy handed Edward a sealed letter. 'I didn't see much point in openin' it.'

Edward ripped open the letter and read the contents to Tommy.

Dear Mr Bell, I am pleased to inform you that your late Aunt, Mary Bell, named you as a beneficiary in her last will and testament. Now that you have reached the age of twenty-one years, you are of age to inherit the property that she left to you, which is Hawthorn Cottage situated in Silksworth Woods and all the goods and chattels remaining within it, the stable, and the parcels of land to the front and rear of the property within the clearing known as Hawthorn Gap. You are now the legal owner of Hawthorn Cottage. The deeds to the property are enclosed. Please keep the deeds in a safe place, as you may need them to prove legal ownership of the property. If I can ever be of service to your good self, please do not hesitate to contact me. Yours sincerely, Mr H Travis, Solicitor.

How about that, Tommy? You own the cottage!'

Tommy grinned and hugged Edward.

'Did you know about this?' he asked.

'I had no idea. Mr Travis must have dealt with this himself.'

'Does he know where you live?' asked Tommy.

Edward hesitated briefly before saying, 'I must have given him this address when I started my employment there. I wonder if he's made the connection.'

He was sure that Mr Travis would have said something to him if he had.

'I wonder,' said Tommy pensively. 'Anyway, eat your broth before it gets cold.'

The men set out for West Herrington at around ten o'clock that evening. They had chosen a large detached house surrounded by trees that couldn't be seen from any roads or dwellings. The house owner was reputed to be miserly, having acquired his wealth through his frugality, and never willingly contributed to charitable causes.

To Edward's surprise, a few delicate snowflakes began to fall as they walked along the road.

'It's a bit early for snow, isn't it?' asked Tommy as they approached the unlit building.

'Perhaps,' said Edward, watching the snowfall.

Before long, the fine flakes gave way to larger flakes that settled on the frozen ground. At the gate to the house, Edward looked back at the tracks they'd left in their wake.

'We should turn back,' he said

'But we're here now,' said Tommy, reaching for the latch on the gate. 'We might as well take somethin' back with us.'

'Tommy!' Edward grabbed his arm to stop him from going any further. Whispering, he pointed at their footprints and said, 'We can't take anything from this house tonight. Our tracks will lead the owner and the police right to us. We must leave now.'

Tommy shook his head. 'Aye, I know you're right. It's just a shame when we're almost on the doorstep.'

'Come on, the inn will still be open in the village. I'll buy you a drink on the way home.'

The following morning, Edward waded through ankle-deep snow on his way to Sunderland, where he ordered a tailored coat, a fine waistcoat, a pair of light-coloured breeches, a finely knitted pair of socks, a pair of black shoes with silver buckles and a cocked hat. The outfit was ready to collect the following week, and Edward was delighted with it.

Unfortunately, he could not visit the orphanage before Christmas as he had planned because the snow began to fall in earnest that week, and the bad weather seemed set to continue for quite some time.

Chapter 16

The Orphanage, Sunderland
March 1767

Edward adjusted his hat, straightened his well-cut coat and lifted his stick to knock on the wooden door—three taps in rapid succession. The young woman who had taken in the orphaned girls opened the door. He hoped she wouldn't recognise him now that he was dressed as a gentleman.

'Good morning! I've come to see Mr Dunsmore. Is he available?'

His eyes scanned her from head to foot. Her plain, prim clothes and cap hid a pretty, young brunette with high cheekbones and a too-slim body. Her green eyes were intelligent and friendly, and he was pleased that they showed no signs of recognition.

'Please, sir, come in. I'll let Mr Dunsmore know you're here,' she said, lowering her gaze.

Edward followed her through the dark corridor until she stopped by a familiar door. He was thankful that it wasn't Mr Kelly who sat behind it anymore.

'Please, wait here,' she said.

The woman knocked at the office door and opened it, and

as she entered the room, the strong scent of tobacco wafted into the hallway, filling Edward's nostrils, and he heard her speaking with a man whose broad Scottish accent sounded harsh to his ears.

A moment later, the rotund Scotsman was facing him and held out a hand in greeting.

'It's verra good of you to pay us a visit at our institution, Mr—'

'Earle.'

'Oh, my goodness! I apologise for ma mistake, your Lordship. Please, come into ma humble office and tek' a seat.'

Edward's eyes sparkled with amusement at the man's false assumption that he was an earl, an English nobleman, but he wouldn't correct him; the error might work in his favour.

The office was large and elaborately decorated, entirely at odds with the rest of the building, and he sat in the proffered chair, smiling graciously.

'I'm sure we're both busy men, Mr Dunsmore,' said Edward, 'so I will get straight to the point. I have just come of age and have discovered that I'm a wealthy man, and I would like to be a benefactor to this orphanage. An anonymous benefactor.'

'Well, thank you, your Lordship. That's verra generous of you. Verra generous, indeed. The world needs more philanthropists like yoursel',' said Mr Dunsmore, raising his eyebrows.

'I will visit when I'm in town,' continued Edward, 'and deposit the funds with you personally. However, I must have your assurance that every penny of it will be spent on the children housed in this establishment, and not for any other purpose and that my donations will be recorded as being received from an anonymous donor.'

'You have ma word, your Lordship. Thank you,' said Alexander Dunsmore, smiling broadly. Edward rose from his chair, and Mr Dunsmore followed his lead. The men shook hands, and then Mr Dunsmore went to the door and shouted, 'Sarah!'

The young woman returned to show Edward out.

'Thank you, Sarah,' said Edward as they reached the outer door, noticing her smile at his use of her name. He turned and nodded to her before walking away.

As Edward strolled down the street, he doubted that all of his money would be used to help the children. It was clear that Mr Dunsmore liked his comforts. However, he was sure his donations would remain anonymous, for the Scotsman had no idea who he was, having not asked for his name or title.

He knew he should laugh at the thought of Edward Earle from Rookhope having a title, but instead, the bitterness that was buried deep inside him came to the surface.

There is so much injustice in the world.

He lengthened his stride and marched through the town. He needed to return to the little cottage in the woods as quickly as possible and change back into his everyday clothes, and then he'd ask Tommy to accompany him to the Coach and Horses for a drink. His friend could always cheer him up.

When he reached the cottage, he hurriedly changed his clothes, stored the outfit in the roof space above the stable, and went to find Tommy. He followed the sound of an axe chopping wood and found his friend cutting down a spindly tree with a curved trunk.

'Hello, Tommy,' he called.

Tommy put down the axe and mopped his brow with his

sleeve.

'I didn't know you were working today,' said Edward.

'I'm not. This one is for us. It would never have made a good tree, fightin' for light like it was. Anyway, how did it go at the orphanage?'

'I'll tell you all about it over a pint.'

'Sounds good. I could do with a wash first though,' said Tommy. 'I'm sweating like a pig.'

The men returned to the cottage and were shocked to see an elderly man standing at their door.

'Hello,' said Tommy. 'Can I help you?'

'Ah! There you are,' said the man as he turned to face them. 'You know, I never knew this cottage was here.'

'What is your interest in this cottage?' asked Edward.

'Oh, I should introduce myself as you clearly have no idea who I am, which goes to show that my visit is absolutely necessary. Reverend Oliver Plunkett at your service.' The vicar nodded at each of them. 'May I come inside?'

'We were just about to go out,' said Tommy.

'This won't take long, I promise you.'

The vicar opened the door and stepped into their home.

Edward and Tommy followed him inside and watched him sit down in the old armchair.

'It's rather a long walk up here and my legs aren't as young as they once were. Now, to the purpose of my visit. Mr Travis mentioned that this cottage had recently come under new ownership and I told him that I hadn't seen anyone new attending my services at St Michael's.' Looking at the sparsely furnished room, the vicar asked, 'Have you just moved here?'

'No, we've lived here for ages,' said Tommy.

'Is it just the two of you who live here?'

'Aye, just me and Edward.'

Edward looked daggers at Tommy for using his name, and Tommy lowered his eyes.

'May I ask why neither of you has been to church yet? Perhaps you don't know where it is?'

'Reverend,' said Edward. 'With all due respect, we won't be attending your church now or in the future.'

'And why is that, may I ask?' asked the vicar, sounding affronted.

'We spent a lot of time praying when we were children but God never helped us when we needed him, so why would we go now when we don't need his help anymore?'

'I assume you know it's compulsory to attend church at least twice a year.'

'That will not affect our decision, Reverend. Now, if you don't mind, we were about to go out.'

Edward opened the door to show him out.

The vicar stood up and stepped over to the doorway, stopping and turning back to face them.

'Everybody in this world is a sinner and everybody is in need of God's help. You mark my words.'

When the door closed, Edward sighed heavily.

'Come on,' said Tommy. 'Let's go and have that drink.'

Chapter 17

Sunderland Town
July 1767

Carrying a large sack over his shoulder, Edward walked furtively down the narrow alley and climbed the steps to the upstairs room he had been discreetly visiting for the last year or so. He looked around to ensure he was not being watched and knocked three times. When a young man opened the door, Edward rushed inside.

An older man with scruffy white hair sat at the table.

'What have you got for us tonight?' asked Will Bennett, staring at Edward's haul. 'Tip it out onto the table. Don't be shy.'

Edward didn't want to damage the silverware, so he carefully removed each piece and placed them in front of Will.

As Will picked up each one in turn, he screwed up his eyes to read the hallmarks and estimated its weight in his hand.

'Another nice collection, you've brought us,' he said. 'I think we'll get about six pounds for this lot, so that's four pounds for you and two pounds for us.'

Will counted the bank notes and handed them to Edward, who put them in his coat pocket.

'You know, you're gettin' rather good at this,' said Will. 'Perhaps too good.'

'What do you mean by that?' asked Edward.

'Well, there's only a certain amount of silver that can pass through our hands without attracting notice from the authorities and suchlike. Each time you come in here with more and more stuff, and that's not good for us. If you want us to take your silver from now on, the price will have to go up.'

Edward wondered if Will was telling the truth or if this was just a ploy for the Bennetts to make more money out of him.

'How much more?' asked Edward.

'You get half. We get half.' Will looked into Edward's eyes without blinking, waiting to see if Edward would agree to the new terms.

'Half!' gasped Edward. 'That hardly seems fair.'

'Everyone takes a risk in this game. You when you steal. Us when we move the stuff on. It seems fair enough to me.'

'I'll think about it,' said Edward.

He remembered the warning he had received about doing business with the Bennetts and acted cannily. He had no intention of giving these crooks half of the proceeds from his thieving, but he decided that telling them that might not be wise. He would look elsewhere for ways to dispose of the stolen silver.

Wanting to leave on good terms, Edward said, 'Thank you, Will. Good doing business with you again.'

The men shook hands, and Edward made for the door, glad that neither of the men prevented him from leaving the room.

Chapter 18

The Orphanage, Sunderland
December 1767

'I've given regular donations to this orphanage for nine months now,' said Edward, 'and I would like to know how my money has benefited the children.'

Alexander Dunsmore leaned back in his chair and took an ornately carved pipe from the top drawer of his desk. He rose to his feet, lit a taper from the coal fire in his office, held it to the tobacco in the pipe bowl, puffing wildly until it was lit, and then threw the taper into the fire.

Edward scrutinised Mr Dunsmore's every move, suspicious that he may have taken the money himself. When Edward entered the office, he'd noticed it had been newly refurbished, and Dunsmore's fashionable clothes appeared new, too.

'I can assure you that the orphans have benefited greatly frae your generosity. Why don't you come and see frae yoursel'?' said Mr Dunsmore. 'On Christmas day, you'd be welcome to come and have your dinner wi' us and observe the weans first hand. They'll be eatin' the same food as us, and each of them will receive a gift this year. I don't believe that has ever happened before, not when funds were in short supply. Why not come along and see what a difference your donations are makin' to the children?'

Not sure if Mr Dunsmore was bluffing, Edward said, 'What an excellent idea! I would be delighted to spend Christmas here with the children. I will have a manservant with me. I hope he'll be welcome to join us? If I'm satisfied that the children are in fact benefiting from my payments, you will continue to receive them. If there are any doubts in my mind whatsoever, then the payments will stop. Do I make myself clear?'

'Aye, my Lord. Verra clear. I can assure you that you'll nae be disappointed.'

Edward nodded and left the office, pleased that he had secured a Christmas dinner for both Tommy and himself.

On Christmas day, Edward and Tommy washed and dressed in their best clothes before walking into Sunderland.

'Don't forget to call me sir when you speak to me, and we can't go too far wrong,' said Edward.

Tommy pulled at his collar. 'I hope you're right. You've taken to bein' a gentleman like a duck to water, but I don't know, it doesn't feel right to me, pretendin' to be somebody else. '

'You'll still be Tommy. If anyone asks your surname, give them a different name. Don't say Tommy Bell.'

Tommy nodded.

'If they ask where you're from, be vague, and say something like beyond Durham.'

Tommy shook his head. 'I'll never remember all that. Can I just make somethin' up?'

'Aye, Tommy, you can,' said Edward, knowing his friend might struggle to keep up the pretence, but it was worth the risk for a Christmas dinner. His mouth was watering just thinking about it. 'Just remember that you're my servant. That's the most important thing.'

Mr Dunsmore welcomed the men to the orphanage and showed them straight into the dining room, where the children sat in their Sunday clothes, waiting for their lunch.

'This brings back memories,' whispered Tommy.

They followed Mr Dunsmore to an empty table at the far end of the room, by the window, and sat down.

'My wife is supervising in the kitchen. Sarah and some of the lasses will serve the food shortly. Would you care for some wine while we wait?'

'No, thank you. Water will suffice.' Edward wanted to keep his wits about him.

'And for your man? What's your name, laddie?'

'Thomas Lightbottom,' replied Tommy, the falsehood slipping easily from his lips.

Edward covered his laugh with a fake cough.

'I'll get that water for you.' Mr Dunsmore took an empty glass from the table and went to the kitchen.

'Lightbottom!' said Edward. 'Where on earth did that name come from?'

Tommy shrugged. 'It was the first name I thought of.'

Edward would never understand how Tommy's mind worked, but he loved that his friend could still surprise him after all the years they had known each other.

Mr Dunsmore returned with the filled glass and put it on the table before Edward. By his side stood a lady in an elegant dress.

'I'd like to introduce ma wife, Mrs Elizabeth Dunsmore.'

Mr Dunsmore hesitated when he realised he did not know

his benefactor's name, and his cheeks flushed.

'Call me Edward,' said Edward, with a friendly smile.

Giving my first name can't hurt, can it?

He stood up, took her gloved hand and kissed it. 'I'm delighted to make your acquaintance, ma'am.'

Tommy nodded and smiled up at her. 'Likewise,' he said.

They all sat silently at the table as several girls served them first, followed by the children, and then took their seats.

Mr Dunsmore put his hands together and closed his eyes. The children followed his lead, and they recited grace together before eating.

Edward's mind was filled with memories from his childhood at the institution, good times and bad, but in all his time there, he had never had a dinner like this. On his plate were two slices of roast beef, parsnips, Brussels sprouts, carrots, turnips, potatoes and gravy. It was the most delicious meal that he had ever tasted.

'The food is excellent,' he said.

Mrs Dunsmore smiled at the compliment and said, 'Thank you.' Looking him in the eyes, she said, 'And thank you! After all, it was you that made this possible.'

Edward was dismayed that Mr Dunsmore had confided in his wife that he was contributing to the orphanage and glared at the man. Mr Dunsmore's face reddened, and he shifted uncomfortably under Edward's gaze.

He considered leaving right away or refusing to make any more payments to the orphanage and marching to the door, but he didn't want to make a scene and spoil the best Christmas these children were likely to have had. He decided it would be better to privately mention the indiscretion to Mr Dunsmore at their next meeting and reiterate that nobody else should know about his 'anonymous' donations.

'You're very welcome, Mrs Dunsmore, and so are the children,' said Edward calmly. He turned to watch the children wolfing down the food, knowing they were unlikely to have eaten so well in their lives. It was thrilling to think that he had made this possible. If there had ever been any doubt about how he provided for these children, there was none now. Seeing their smiling faces and hearing their laughter justified all of his actions—every single one.

After eating plum pudding, Mr Dunsmore left the room and returned shortly after carrying a large sack, which he brought to their table.

'These are the gifts for the children,' he said to Edward. 'When I call out their names, would you like to hand them their gifts?'

'Honestly, there's no need to involve me,' said Edward, shaking his head. 'Perhaps it would be better for Mrs Dunsmore to do the honours.'

'I'd be more than happy to,' said Mrs Dunsmore, getting to her feet. 'Shall we make a start?'

Every child was called to receive a Christmas present, which they opened when they returned to their seats, unwrapping toys, books, jewellery, handkerchiefs and shawls. Edward could see that the gifts had been individually chosen for each child, and they all looked overjoyed to have something they could call their own.

He saw Sarah watching the children, smiling at their reactions when they opened the packages, and he suspected she had been responsible for choosing and wrapping the gifts.

Edward remembered leaving the orphanage with only his clothes and Dorothy's ribbon. He knew what it was like to have very little and was delighted that his contributions made a difference in these children's lives. He was glad he had accepted Mr Dunsmore's invitation.

Chapter 19

The Orphanage, Sunderland
April 1768

Satisfied that his donations were being used well, Edward returned to the orphanage a few months later to hand over his next payment. While Mr Dunsmore completed the entry in a ledger, Edward stood up and paced the room, still angry at Mr Dunsmore's indiscretion.

'When I first came here,' he said, 'I stipulated very clearly that my donations were to remain anonymous. However, when I attended Christmas lunch, it was clear that you had taken your wife into your confidence. Needless to say, this breach of promise has upset me greatly. I trust that it will not happen again. Nobody else must know that I contribute to the orphanage. Do I make myself clear? If my wishes are not honoured, the payments will stop.'

'Edward, I didnae mean no harm. My wife is a verra clever woman and she guessed the reason for your invitation to our Christmas meal. On my oath, I swear that I will nae tell another soul.'

Edward was standing at the back of the room when the office door burst open, and an immaculately dressed young woman with blonde hair marched into the room.

'Charlotte, dearie, I wasn't expecting you,' said Mr Dunsmore, rising from his seat and looking towards the door. 'Don't you have a chaperone with you?'

'Oh, Alex, you're just like the rest of them. Mother is too busy running the household, and my sisters have married and left home. I am supposed to stay at home and be bored because they're too busy to come shopping with me?'

'You know your mother doesn't like you comin' into town alone.'

Charlotte pouted.

'Please may I wait here until you're ready to leave, Alex, and then you can take me home?'

'It will be at least half an hour before I'm finished for the day.'

Edward noticed the woman glance in his direction.

'Oh, you have a visitor,' she said. 'I'm so sorry to intrude. Won't you introduce us?'

'Of course! Where are ma manners? My Lord, please allow me to introduce Miss Charlotte Liddell, my wife's youngest sister.'

'I'm Edward,' said Edward, kissing her hand. 'It's very nice to meet you.'

'You too.' She held his gaze a little longer than necessary.

'I wonder,' he asked, 'are you connected to the glassmaking Liddells?'

'Yes, my father and uncle own the glassworks by the river.'

Edward smiled. Dunsmore had married into money. That explained the refurbished office and his fashionable dress. The Liddells were one of the wealthiest families in the parish. Edward admired Charlotte's father and uncle because they

107

were self-made men, having worked hard to make their fortune, not simply inherited it like Lord Malham and his sort.

'Edward, as Alex isn't ready to drive me home yet, I wonder if I could impose on you. Would you be so kind as to accompany me to the tearoom just up the street? I would prefer not to go there alone.'

'It would be my pleasure, Miss Liddell.'

Edward bade farewell to Mr Dunsmore, who he thought looked a little smug, puffing at his pipe, as he took Charlotte's arm to escort her to the tearoom.

Charlotte chose a table by the window that looked out onto the road and sat down. As Edward sat opposite her, the sunlight caught her features, and he couldn't help but admire her bright blue eyes, straight nose and flawless pale skin. She was a beautiful woman, one far above the reaches of Edward Earle but well within reach of an actual earl, he thought cynically. He wondered if meeting Charlotte had been accidental or if it had been fabricated by Dunsmore, who was under the false impression that Edward was an earl and, therefore, a very eligible bachelor. It was understandable that he'd want a good marriage for his sister-in-law.

Was Mr Dunsmore trying to match-make?

While he'd been lost in thought, Charlotte had ordered tea, and a waitress delivered a tray to their table.

As Charlotte poured the tea, she said, 'The orphanage is a dreadful place. I would never set foot in it if Alex didn't own it. May I ask why you were there today? Taking on a young servant, perhaps?'

'I'm afraid I can't disclose my business.'

'Oh! A man with secrets.' Charlotte smiled, raising her

eyebrows.

Edward felt a sense of dread at her piqued interest. Yes, he had plenty of secrets, none of which he was prepared to reveal to a woman he'd just met.

'There are many more interesting topics of conversation than me. You, for instance. Tell me about yourself.'

His ruse worked. Charlotte talked about her family, their house in the town and their place in the country, and the governess she'd had as a girl whom she still missed, and listed her many accomplishments until the teapot and cups were empty.

'A refill?' asked Charlotte.

'No, thank you. I've enjoyed your company enormously, but I must be on my way. Shall I walk you back to the orphanage?'

'That's very kind of you. Thank you.'

He helped Charlotte cross the street and knocked at the door with his stick.

Sarah promptly answered it and stepped back awkwardly when she saw Edward standing on the doorstep with Charlotte by his side.

'Miss Liddell is here for Mr Dunsmore,' Edward announced.

'Thank you very much for accompanying me, Edward,' said Charlotte, looking at him through her lashes.

'It was my pleasure.' Edward lifted her hand in his and gently kissed it.

Charlotte entered the building and turned back briefly, smiling warmly at Edward, before she walked away.

Sarah nodded politely and closed the door without saying a word.

As he left, he wondered what he had done to upset her.

Chapter 20

Hawthorn Cottage, Silksworth
May 1768

'We're runnin' out of places to steal from around here,' said Tommy, moving a wooden bucket to catch drips of water that fell through the gaps in the thatched roof. 'There aren't many people with money that live around here.'

'Yes, I know,' said Edward. 'I've wondered about that myself, and I think I know the solution.'

'What's that?' asked Tommy. 'We cannot walk much further than we do now, especially in the summer when it's not dark for very long.'

'There is a way that we could go further afield and carry more.'

Tommy looked intrigued.

'We should get some horses.' Edward raised his eyebrows and waited for his friend's reaction.

'Horses! I've never been on a horse in me life,' said Tommy. 'Can you ride a horse?'

'Yes, I learnt to ride when I was a child, and I managed quite well when I visited Rookhope a few years ago, when I went to Weardale.'

'Aye, I remember. You came back all smitten with a lass. Dorothy, was it?'

Edward blushed slightly at the mention of Dorothy's name.

'Aye, I'm right. It was Dorothy,' said Tommy gleefully. 'You talked about nothin' else for weeks. You were proper love sick.'

'I'll teach you to ride,' said Edward, changing the subject to one he was more comfortable with. 'It's easy once you know how.'

Tommy didn't look convinced but said, 'Aye, alright, if it means I won't have to do as much walkin'. It's wearin' me feet out, never mind me shoes.'

A few days later, Edward and Tommy attended a sale of horses in Newcastle marketplace, with Edward dressed as a gentleman and Tommy as his servant. Edward would need to pay for the animals with cash, and he didn't want anyone to question that it was his money; he had to look the part.

The town was bustling. Farmers, carters, merchants, and gentlemen gathered to examine the livestock on offer. There were horses and ponies of all shapes and sizes, from enormous cart horses that towered above them to children's riding ponies that didn't reach their hips.

Edward felt utterly out of his depth. He'd never looked at a horse before with a view to buying it. He wished John or Mr Robson was there to advise him. He tried to recall the few things he'd heard them say about horses, such as that having long teeth meant they were old.

How long should their teeth be? And how do you get them to open their mouths to look inside?

It was common sense, he thought, to avoid the horses that were so thin that their ribs showed and the fat ones that looked lazy. Edward concentrated on the ones that looked like the horses he'd seen gentlemen ride—tall, lean animals with intelligent eyes.

He saw a grey horse he admired and asked the seller to tell him about it.

'This mare's ten years old,' he replied. He quickly opened her mouth and showed them her teeth as proof of her age. 'She's been a lady's mount for leisure riding and hunting. She's an easy ride, and she has stamina. I've seen her out on the hunt all day and still look fresh when she's come back to the stable.'

'How much are you asking for her?' asked Edward. He liked what he had heard and thought she might be a good horse for Tommy. She appeared gentle and kind.

'Four pounds.'

'If you'll accept three pounds and ten shillings, I'll take her.'

'Thank you, sir, that would be acceptable.' He held out his hand to shake on the deal. 'Ghost, she's called, 'cos she quiet. She can sneak up behind you in the field, and you'll not know she's there.'

Edward counted out the cash and handed it to the stableman.

'Thank you,' he replied, handing the mare's reins to Tommy, who hesitated to take them, having never held a horse before.

Edward nodded as he left, thinking she was perfect for their needs—a quiet horse with stamina for sneaking around at night.

As they moved away, Edward said, 'Keep a tight hold of the leather straps, Tommy. Don't let loose, whatever you do.'

Another horse caught Edward's attention on the same row, and he stood back to admire it. Another mare, if he was correct. She was a few inches taller than the grey. Her coat was dark chestnut, and it shone magnificently in the sunlight, and she had a white star on her forehead. She was a beauty.

'Tell me about this horse,' he said to its handler.

'This here is Brandy. She's just turned six years old. Been working as a gentleman's hunter up in Northumberland. Lovely mover. She's fast, very fast and will jump anythin' that's in her way. Once she's goin', there's no stoppin' her.'

'Why is the gentleman selling her?'

'He passed away, suddenly, about a month back.'

'I'm sorry to hear that,' said Edward, thinking there couldn't be a more genuine reason for selling the animal.

'How much are you asking for her?'

'Five pounds.'

Edward flinched. He looked over the horse again, and his head was telling him that he shouldn't buy her because it would leave him with little money to spare, but his heart was telling him that this was the horse for him.

'Would you accept four pounds?'

The handler hesitated before saying, 'The widow was hoping for the full price. Could you go to four pounds and fifteen shillings? The tack is included in the sale and it's almost new. That's got to be worth at least fifteen shillings.'

'You have a deal,' Edward held out his hand, and the man shook it.

'And you, sir, have bought the best horse at this market.'

He took the reins and led her away, thinking the handler was speaking the truth. He thought she was among the best riding horses he'd ever seen.

Edward bought a second-hand saddle for Tommy's horse, and they set off for home.

After they'd walked over the old stone bridge that crossed the River Tyne, Edward said, 'It's too far to walk all the way back to Silksworth. We'll have to ride. I'll help you up. All you need to do is sit there and hold on to her mane.'

Tommy's eyes were wide, and his voice trembled when he said, 'I don't know why we came all this way to get horses. We could have got them from the dealer in Sunderland, or somewhere closer than Newcastle anyway.'

'If we bought local horses, someone might recognise them,' said Edward.

'Ah! I would never have thought of that. You always think of everythin', you do.'

'Bend your left knee,' said Edward. 'When I lift you up, swing your right leg over and sit on the saddle.'

When Tommy was astride Ghost with his feet in the stirrups, Edward reminded him to hold on to her mane with both hands. He then mounted his horse, which pranced around on the spot for a few moments, eager to go, but he held her back.

Seeing the look of horror on Tommy's face, Edward said, 'I'm holding Ghost's reins so she'll follow me. We'll go slowly until you get used to it.'

They rode home slowly, and night had fallen by the time they finally returned to the cottage. They both ached from riding for so long.

'I don't think me legs will ever be straight again,' said Tommy, walking bow-legged to the door. 'And me backside's as sore as hell.'

Edward untacked the horses, led them to the stable and ensured they had hay and water, thinking that he and Tommy would need a lot of practice on the horses before taking them out at night.

Chapter 21

White Hall Farm, Rookhope
June 1768

The sun was low in the sky when Edward Earle pulled up his horse outside White Hall Farm at Rookhope and dismounted.

The farmhouse door opened, and a young man stepped outside to see who was there. When he recognised his old friend, his step quickened, and he slapped Edward on the back and greeted him heartily.

'It's been a while since we've seen you, Ed. How have you been?'

'Good, John. Good. How are you? And the family?'

'We're all well, thank you. Father's gettin' on a bit and he's supposed to be retired now, but the old man doesn't know the meanin' of the word. He still comes to the smelt mill every day and bosses me about!'

Edward removed the saddle from his mare and walked her towards a gate, where he removed her bridle and released her into a field to graze and rest for the night. He took the tack into the barn.

'Nice horse you have there,' said John, admiring the mare.

'Yes, she's a beauty,' replied Edward. 'And Dorothy? How is

she?'

'Our Dot, she's alright. She still asks about you.'

Edward felt a lump in his throat. When he left Rookhope after his last visit, it was Dorothy whom he'd missed the most. If he'd taken another path in life, he would have returned sooner and married her, but it was too late to do that now that he was a thief—he was no longer worthy of being her husband.

'Come on in,' said John. 'They'll all want to see you.'

The Robsons' kitchen was exactly how it had always been. Warm, inviting, and full of familiar faces that turned to look at him when he entered.

'Come on in, lad, and take the weight off them feet,' said Mrs Robson. 'Have you had anythin' to eat?' Without waiting for a reply, she continued, 'You'll have a bit of tatie cake, won't you? What do you want with it? Tea? Milk?'

'Stop your fussin', Mother,' said John. 'He doesn't want milk. He's not a bairn. He'll have a piece of tatie cake and some ale.'

'I'll fuss as long as I'm livin', son,' Mrs Robson scolded. 'It's not often we get visitors in this house, and I'll not have anyone say they didn't get a good feed when they were here.'

Edward sat in a vacant chair at the table, watched by the younger children. He had been aware of Dorothy's absence as soon as he'd entered the house and idly wondered where she could be.

'So, what have you come for this time?' asked Mr Robson, sitting by the fire smoking his long clay pipe.

'He's a friend of the family, Father,' said John. 'He doesn't need a reason to come and see us. If things had been different, this would have been his home.'

'Don't start on that, John,' said Mrs Robson. 'We couldn't

take him in when his mother passed. There were twelve of us in this house and our Elizabeth was on the way, God rest her soul.' She put a plate and mug on the table in front of Edward. 'I've been sorry about it ever since, but we just couldn't. I know this place is called White Hall Farm, but I don't know where the Hall bit of the name comes from. We had two rooms upstairs and two rooms downstairs, and they were full to the brim. Your father was workin' at the smelt mill six days a week and runnin' this farm an' all, just to make ends meet. So, we'll hear no more about it, do you hear?'

Mrs Robson's tirade silenced her son.

After Edward had eaten, he thanked Mrs Robson and asked John if he'd like to go to the inn at Stotsfieldburn, and he was relieved when John agreed. There was something he wanted to speak to him about privately, and there was no chance of that happening at the farm—there was always somebody within hearing distance.

It was a warm, pleasant evening for a walk to the village. The track was dry and dusty after the long, hot summer.

'I was hoping to ask a favour of you,' said Edward.

'So, Father was right,' John laughed. 'There was a reason for you comin' to see us.'

'Yes, I'm afraid so. I've known you for a long time and know you can keep a secret. What I'm going to tell you, I want to go no further, whether or not you take me up on my offer. Can you agree to that?'

'Of course, I can.'

'Where to start?' Edward paused, looking for the right words. 'If I needed some silver melting down, could you do it for me? Obviously, I'd make it worth your while.'

John came to a sudden halt. 'What have you got yourself

into?' he asked.

'I'd rather not say, if you don't mind.'

'If I don't mind,' sneered John. 'Of course, I bloody mind. I need to know what I'm gettin' meself into.'

They stood in the middle of the secluded track, looking at one another. Except for Tommy, who knew everything about him, John was the person Edward trusted the most. That was why he was here.

Would John keep his mouth shut when he knew the silver was stolen?

Knowing he had little choice but to tell John what he was doing and why, he told his friend the whole story, from meeting his father when he was eighteen to the Bennetts increasing their share for disposing of his silverware.

John stood shaking his head. 'I don't know, Ed. I could get into a lot of trouble for that, and me Father has eyes like a hawk. He doesn't miss a thing.'

While John was deep in thought, Edward stood patiently waiting for a reply.

'Would it just be the once or a regular thing?'

'Every couple of months. The extra money could help you to get your own place.'

'Aye, that's true,' said John. 'Jenny's desperate for us to get married, but I can't take a wife into our house. Like me mother said, there's not enough room for all that lives there. We're trippin' over ourselves as it is.'

'I know it's a lot to ask,' said Edward. 'Have a think about it and let me know.'

'Aye, alright. By the way, I hope you don't mind sleepin' in the barn tonight?'

'Have I ever minded sleeping in the barn?'

John laughed loudly. 'You know, I begged me Mother to let you live in it after what happened, but she was right as usual. It would never have worked out in the wintertime.'

'Your family would have taken me in if they could, John, I know that. I don't bear them any grudges.'

John slapped Edward on the back again and said, 'Come on, let's get those pints in before the pub closes.'

Early the following day, Edward was woken by birdsong. He sat up, brushed the hay out of his hair and yawned as he stretched.

'Good morning, Edward.'

Edward's eyes searched the barn and the farmyard for the young woman whose voice he would recognise anywhere. She was standing by the well, filling a pail with water, but her eyes were fixed on him.

He got up and crossed the yard to see her.

'Dorothy, you're looking well.'

'Thank you,' she said shyly. 'You look good an' all.' Reaching up, she removed a piece of hay from his hair.

'Are you courting?'

Edward wanted to drop his head into his hands. *Why did I ask that?* He had no right. *What business is it of mine if she's seeing another man?*

'No, I'm not courtin',' she said firmly, and Edward knew that she was waiting for him to ask her out, but he couldn't. Not now.

Dorothy remembered him as the boy she'd known and loved all those years ago. She didn't know the real Edward Earle, the man of contradictions—the clerk, the thief and the benefactor. And as with Charlotte Liddell, he could never let Dorothy know that man.

'It's lovely to see you again, Dorothy,' he said. 'Is your John about?'

Her smile faded at his dismissal, and she said quietly, 'Aye, you'll find him in the byre.'

With a heavy heart, Edward strolled to the byre, reflecting on his childhood. His late mother's cottage was on the Robsons' land, and he'd spent so much time at the farm with John and Dorothy when he was growing up that he might as well have lived there.

White Hall Farm felt like home, yet coming back inevitably made him sad. He wasn't sure if it was because his mother had died there at the age of twenty-nine, leaving him an orphan, or if it was discovering who his father was after her death, or if it was because he had been denied a place in the Robson household, or if it was regret that he could never be with Dorothy, his first love.

Perhaps it's all of these things.

In the byre, John was seated on a small stool, milking the cow, streams of white liquid sloshing rhythmically into a metal pail. He glanced up when Edward stood in the doorway, blocking the light.

'Ed. You're up. We'll away in and have some breakfast when I'm done here.'

'That sounds good, thank you.' Whispering, he said, 'Have you thought any more about what I said last night?'

'Aye, I have. I couldn't do it at Rookhope cos' me Father would be on to us in no time, but I've heard they're hirin' smelters at Nenthead. I'll have a ride over one day and see what the crack is.'

Edward touched John's shoulder and said, 'Thank you.'

'I'm not makin' any promises, mind you.'

'I know that John, but I'm glad that you're at least considering it. I thought your conscience might get the better of you with you being a church-going fellow.'

'Don't you go to church anymore?'

'No. I don't see the point in it,' said Edward. 'You can do good and help others without going to church every Sunday and listening to a preacher drone on and on.'

John laughed. 'If that's what you think, you should listen to John Wesley preachin'. He believes that you can pray to God anywhere, and he does. His sermons are out in the open air, and people crowd around to hear him. There's a lot of folks in Weardale have turned their backs on the church and go to Wesley-style prayer meetings in each other's houses instead, or in their gardens if the weather's nice.'

'Sounds like this Wesley fellow has the right idea,' said Edward.

Standing up and lifting the pail, John said, 'Let's go and get somethin' to eat. I'm hungry this mornin'.'

Edward followed John to the farmhouse, hoping he wouldn't regret involving his friend in his scheme. What they were doing was illegal and dangerous, and by helping him, John was taking a considerable risk.

Chapter 22

Durham Gaol
October 1770

On the third day that Edward and Tommy were in gaol, Edward was still brooding over who could have betrayed them.

First on his list were John Robson and his wife, Jenny. They knew he was a highwayman and lived near Silksworth, but they didn't know the exact location of the cottage. He was confident that his old friend wouldn't have given him up because by doing so, he would implicate himself, too.

Next on the list were the Bennett brothers, Johnny and Will, who fenced his stolen goods. They were in a similar predicament to John, although they could have paid someone to inform the police on their behalf. *Could they have done it out of revenge because I took the silver elsewhere, even though I continued to use them to fence jewellery?* The Bennetts didn't know where he lived. *Unless they followed me home one night.* They were certainly capable of doing that; they were shady characters at best and downright villains at worst. Nothing they did would surprise him.

And then there was Sarah Potts from the orphanage. She

knew he and Tommy were highwaymen and where they lived—and she was a woman. The constable had said a woman had given him their details. But he'd trusted Sarah implicitly and couldn't understand why she would have betrayed them after all this time.

Suddenly, he recalled the look on Sarah's face when he was with Charlotte. *Could Sarah be jealous?* He wasn't sure, but if he were right in his assumption that Sarah was jealous of Charlotte, that would give her a motive, too. He had always been fond of Sarah in a sisterly fashion, and the idea of her betrayal hurt him deeply.

'There's only one person who knows what we do and where we live,' said Edward.

'Who's that?' asked Tommy.

'Sarah Potts.'

Tommy's eyes widened. 'She wouldn't have told on us. Never! She just wouldn't.'

'I've thought about this a lot, Tommy. It can't be anyone else. Don't you see? She's the only one who could have told them where we live. But I have no idea why she did it.'

'I'm not havin' it, Edward. It wasn't her. No way!'

'Shush! You can't raise your voice here. We might be overheard.'

Tommy punched the iron bars and yelled. He held his bleeding knuckles against his chest and glowered at Edward.

A guard came to their cell door. 'Edward Earle? Thomas Bell?' he asked, looking from one to the other.

Edward nodded.

'I've got some news for you,' said the guard. 'A man is comin' in this afternoon to see if you are the highwaymen that robbed him. He saw the piece in the newspaper yesterday. When he gets here, the guards will come and take you up the yard to be identified.' Raising his eyebrows, he said, 'And don't think about makin' a run for it. You'll both be handcuffed and shackled.'

The man turned away and left.

Tommy was shaking. 'That's it. We're done for.'

Edward stood in front of his friend, held him by the arms, and said, 'Tommy, listen to me.'

Edward waited until Tommy looked at him so he knew he was listening.

'The man might not be someone we robbed. Even if we did, he might not recognise us. This is important. When we go up there, you must stay calm. If you're shaking or sweating, it will make you look guilty. And if you recognise the man, do not show any signs of recognition, do you hear me?'

'Aye,' said Tommy, 'but what if he says it was us?'

'We deny it. We say we've never laid eyes on him before. Can you do that, Tommy? Can you do that for me? I'll be standing right beside you.'

'Aye, I think so.'

Edward sighed and hugged his friend. 'Thank you,' he whispered.

Outwardly, Edward appeared calm, but during the next few hours, while he waited for the guards to come, he felt fear like he had never felt before. He couldn't eat. He couldn't think. He stretched to relieve the tension in his muscles and forced himself to breathe more deeply, which was difficult when the air inside the gaol was so putrid.

'Do you regret what we did?' asked Tommy.

'I don't know.'

Edward thought about the question. Working as a clerk by

day, planning burglaries, stealing by night, and impersonating a gentleman benefactor now and again, he'd never had time to reflect on his life before. *Do I regret what we've done?*

He had regrets, yes. He regretted the fear that he had caused their victims, the harm that had come to Tommy, and all the lies and deceit. Looking back, he was ashamed of his actions. But he did not regret that he had made the lives of many young orphans more bearable.

It was mid-afternoon before the guards appeared at the cell door carrying handcuffs and shackles. They unlocked the door, shackled the prisoners' feet together and then handcuffed Edward's wrist to Tommy's.

They walked slowly through the dark passage, chains jangling, with one guard leading the way and another following.

Edward blinked as they entered the yard, and the sunlight hurt his eyes. He raised his untethered hand to shield his face and noticed Tommy was looking down at the ground to avoid the glare.

'Stand still,' said the guard. 'No talkin' to the witness unless spoken to. And behave yourselves.'

They stood in the yard and waited until two well-dressed men and a policeman approached them.

One of the men came closer, scrutinised their faces, and stepped back. He whispered something to the policeman. Edward was unable to hear what he said.

'The gentleman would like to hear your voice,' the policeman said to Edward. 'Can you say somethin' to him?'

'Good afternoon. I trust you had a pleasant journey here. I hope the prison management offered you refreshments on your arrival.' Edward purposefully put on his politest voice, which would not have been out of place in the best houses in the country. He would never have used this voice when thieving.

The man shook his head and said to the others, 'This is definitely not the man that robbed me. There's a similarity in his build, but the voice is nothing like him. I'm afraid you've arrested the wrong man.'

Edward was heartened by his words and wondered if he and Tommy might be released, but his joy was short-lived. The man who had been quiet throughout the process came forward and stood in front of Edward. 'That's just the first one, Earle. There'll be more. We'll keep you here until one of them identifies you as a highwayman. It'll happen soon enough. Then, you'll get what you deserve.' Looking at Tommy, he said, 'You an' all.'

The men left, and the guards accompanied Edward and Tommy back to the cell, removed their restraints, and locked the door behind them.

Tommy sat on the edge of the bed, silent tears pouring down his face. Edward sat next to him and put an arm around his shoulder.

It was Edward's turn to think that they were done for.

Chapter 23

Sunderland Town
August 1770

Edward Earle wore his gentleman's outfit and strode through the town as though he owned it. He looked and felt like an aristocrat walking tall and strolling confidently along the sun-drenched streets.

As he passed a jeweller's shop, he glanced in the window and recognised several pieces of jewellery he had acquired from a stately home near Houghton-le-Spring. He surmised that the jewellers must have bought them from the Bennetts or their associates.

An elegant woman carrying several packages exited the shop, and he recognised her immediately as Charlotte Liddell. To walk past when he knew she'd seen him would have been the height of bad manners. Glad he was wearing his gentleman's clothing, he stopped to pass the time of day.

'Miss Liddell, how lovely to see you again.'

'And you too, Edward.'

Seeing that she was unaccompanied, he asked, 'Where are you headed?'

'I've finished my business in town, so I'm going to the

orphanage. I hope Alex will be kind enough to take me home.'

'What a coincidence! That's where I'm going,' Edward smiled. 'Perhaps I might accompany you?'

'Thank you.' She smiled up at him sweetly.

Edward took the packages that she carried, placed them under one arm, and held out the other, and she took it without hesitation.

As they passed a greengrocer's shop, Edward glanced at their reflection in the large shop window. He hardly recognised himself. He appeared to be a perfect suitor for the young lady by his side, with his long, tightly fitting brown coat and waistcoat, light breeches and shiny black shoes with silver buckles. His dark brown hair was tied back with Dorothy's black ribbon and looked very tidy.

How deceptive appearances could be, he thought. He was definitely not the perfect suitor for a woman like Charlotte Liddell.

While they walked, they chatted amiably, or rather, he let Charlotte talk because he was uncertain what to say. Feeling every bit the imposter, he dared not speak about himself in case he revealed something he shouldn't—spending time in Miss Liddell's company was proving to be tricky.

He was concentrating so hard on the conversation that he failed to see Sarah Potts wandering behind them, watching their every move.

'Actually,' said Charlotte, 'I hoped I might bump into you today. I've been invited to a ball by a close lady friend. It's at Mosley House in Newcastle. Her family is acquainted with many young ladies but few young gentlemen. She is concerned that there will be a glut of young ladies at the ball with no dancing partners. Would you do me the honour of attending as my guest?'

Edward was unfamiliar with how the upper classes courted but assumed the gentleman would make the first advance, and he thought Charlotte's proposal was very forward, considering she scarcely knew him. In fact, she knew nothing about him except for his name, and only his first name at that.

Has Mr Dunsmore told her more about me?

'I'm very flattered, Miss Liddell, but I must refuse. I have another engagement this weekend.'

'Oh, how disappointing,' she pouted her pretty pink lips. 'Perhaps another time?'

Edward avoided her gaze and said, 'Perhaps.'

At the orphanage, Miss Liddell waited in the corridor while Edward went into Mr Dunsmore's office to give him another donation, and when he came out, he bade her farewell. She held out her hand, and he kissed it, and then, quite unexpectedly, she reached up and kissed him tenderly on the cheek.

Out of the corner of his eye, Edward spotted Sarah walking towards them, looking at him coldly, and by her side was Reverend Plunkett, the vicar who had visited Hawthorn Cottage, his eyebrows drawn, no doubt trying to place him. Edward avoided looking in their direction. He lowered his head and kissed Charlotte's cheek to hide his face from the clergyman as he passed, not caring if he and Charlotte looked like they were lovers. Anything was better than being recognised as the man from Silksworth Woods when he was at the orphanage.

Charlotte put her hand on Edward's cheek and smiled up at him. He recognised her look as an invitation, but he wasn't sure if she wanted him to ask her out or to kiss her again.

'My dear, Edward,' she said, 'Perhaps you're too shy to say how you feel, but as you returned my kiss, I guess you must like me too. That's good enough for now.'

She turned away and entered her brother-in-law's office.

Edward left the building, his mind in a whirl, wondering what he had done to upset Sarah, hoping the vicar wouldn't recognise the gentleman he'd just seen to be the godless man from the woods and fearing that he'd given Charlotte the wrong impression about his feelings for her.

Chapter 24

Wolsingham Show
September 1768

In the early afternoon, Edward arrived at the show field near Wolsingham. He led his mare to the water trough and let her drink, and then he tethered her on a loose rein so she could graze. As he wandered around the show ring, the livestock classes were well underway, but he hadn't come all that way to see the vast array of farm animals and produce on display; he'd come with the sole purpose of speaking with John Robson.

Dorothy was the first of the Robson clan he saw on the show field. She was chatting with a friend and looked radiant in the late summer sun. She wore a pale blue dress, which Edward thought looked lovely against her strawberry blonde hair, which hung down her back in a plait. When she spotted him wandering through the crowd, her face lit up, and she smiled broadly.

'Dorothy,' he said when he reached her, 'you look very well.'
'I am, thank you. How are you?'
'I'm very well, thank you.'
Edward could not take his eyes off her. Her face was milky white, slightly freckled after the summer months, with rosy

cheeks and the most kissable lips.

'It's busy here, isn't it?' she said. 'This is the fifth show and I swear there are more people here every year.'

As she spoke, he watched her lips and had a strong urge to kiss them, but he couldn't, not when there were so many people about. If they had been alone, he would not have been able to resist the temptation.

'Yes, it's busy,' he said.

'We've brought the tup to the show,' she said. 'I'm headin' over that way now. Do you want to come with me?'

'Of course.' He held out his arm, which she took, and they weaved their way through the crowd to the show ring, where they found the rest of the Robson family.

'John, I hoped I'd see you here,' said Edward.

John turned and faced him, 'Ed, it's good to see you again. I wondered if you might turn up today. I suppose you're wantin' an answer to that question.'

Dorothy looked a little puzzled.

'Yes, John,' he said, 'Maybe we should go somewhere a bit quieter to talk.'

Edward led John away from the crowd, and they sat down on the grass at the edge of the field.

'So, what have you decided?' asked Edward, nervously picking at the grass. He desperately needed John's help. If John refused, he would have little choice but to pay the Bennetts the price they were asking, which would mean that he and Tommy would have to steal more often to make up the difference, increasing the risk of being caught.

'I went over to Nent, and it was right that they were takin' on smelters like I'd heard. I had a good look around when I was there. It's a similar layout to the Rookhope mill, but here's a curious thing—there's more silver comin' out of the lead over there than on our side of the hill. I wonder why that is?'

'It could be that there's more silver in the lead ore coming out of the mines over there, or maybe the smelters have a better way of separating the silver from the lead.'

'Aye, it could be one or t'other.' Leaning in conspiratorially, John said, 'Or it could be that they're doin' somethin' else with silver.'

'Do you think so?'

'I don't know. Mebbe. It would account for the difference.'

'What's the manager like at Nenthead?' asked Edward.

'Daniel Beattie. He's a young fella for a manager. Seems a quiet sort.'

'He doesn't sound like the kind of man who would sanction anything underhand.'

'Mebbe he knows nothin' about it,' said John, raising his eyebrows.

'Do you think you could melt down the silver there without him finding out?'

'More chance of that than pullin' the wool over me father's eyes!' John laughed loudly, causing a few eyes to turn in their direction. 'Anyway, I've taken the job.'

'So, you'll do it?' Edward grinned.

'Aye, I'll do it, but for a decent cut. If I get caught, I could end up in gaol—or the American colonies!'

Edward didn't laugh. He knew John was taking a massive risk for him, which could end very badly. 'I'll see you right, John, don't worry about that.'

'The job at Nent comes with a house,' said John. 'I told them I wasn't one for company, and they offered me a cottage standing on its own, on the bank going down from Killhope.

There will be less chance of you bein' seen comin' and goin' up there than in the village.'

'It sounds perfect.'

Edward couldn't believe his luck. Melting down stolen silver at a lead smelting mill was the perfect way to make it disappear.

Silver pieces with identification marks were difficult to pass on because they could be identified as stolen. But a block of solid silver could be sold anywhere without any risk whatsoever of it being traced back to the items from which it had been formed. If any residue of silver was left behind from the process, it could be explained away by the small amounts of silver that occurred naturally within the lead ore. It was the perfect solution.

'And I've got some news,' said John, barely able to contain his excitement. 'Me and Jenny are gettin' married!'

'Congratulations!' Edward grinned. 'I hope you'll be very happy together.'

'You'll come to the weddin', won't you? It's next Saturday, two o'clock at Stanhope.'

'I wouldn't miss it. Getting married, eh? If that's not a cause for a celebration, I don't know what is. Let's go into town, and I'll buy you a beer.'

'Thank you, Ed. That's very good of you.'

As they returned to the horses, Edward looked back at the show field to catch a last glimpse of Dorothy, standing with her father next to the show ring, watching them leave. She smiled and waved.

Edward waved back, glad that he would see her again the following weekend. He mounted his mare and rode away with John.

Chapter 25

St Thomas's Church, Stanhope
September 1768

The marketplace was crowded when Edward arrived at Stanhope the following Saturday. Friends and family of the bride and groom filed up the narrow path to the Norman church.

Edward dismounted and gave a boy in ragged clothing a halfpenny to look after his horse for an hour. Edward stood facing the church dedicated to St Thomas. The last time he'd been there was for his mother's funeral. She was buried under the earth behind it, in a pauper's grave, with no headstone to mark her final resting place. He remembered exactly where her body lay and decided there and then that he would have a stone carved to place on her grave so that she would not be forgotten.

He needed to put his mother's death to the back of his mind today because he was there to celebrate the marriage of John Robson to his childhood sweetheart, Jenny Gardiner.

With a pasted smile, he followed an elderly couple up the path and entered the church, wondering how it could be so cold inside the ancient building when the sun shone brightly outside.

Jimmy Robson, one of John's brothers, ushered Edward to a pew, and he sat down, nodding at the familiar faces that turned his way.

John was sitting in the front row, waiting for his bride, and Edward could see that his friend was nervous. Edward wasn't surprised because he'd heard many tales of brides and grooms being jilted at the altar, and he was relieved that he would never put himself in that vulnerable position. Not only that, marriage was a huge commitment.

How could anyone say they wanted to spend their whole life with one person?

People change. He had changed. The young boy who had sat through his mother's funeral would not recognise the man he had become.

Jenny entered the church looking more beautiful than Edward had ever seen her. She walked up the aisle with her father, followed by two bridesmaids, one of whom was Dorothy. Edward's fake smile suddenly turned into a real one at the sight of her.

A bridesmaid is not supposed to outshine the bride, but in Edward's eyes, Dorothy did. Her strawberry blonde hair had been curled in the fashion of ladies in town, and she wore a dress the colour of violets.

Dorothy looked back over her shoulder at him after she'd passed and smiled, a smile that warmed his heart. He would have made the journey to Stanhope for that smile alone.

He sat quietly during the service and contemplated marriage, not the ceremony but the day-to-day life of living with a spouse, and wondered what he would miss by remaining a bachelor for the rest of his life.

Most of the adults he knew were married, and he wondered if they had married because they wanted to or because it was expected of them. Either way, most of them seemed happy together, although a few constantly bickered. The couple who owned the Coach and Horses, where he and Tommy occasionally had a drink, came to mind.

He thought about how John's life would change from that day on. He would move out of his crowded family home to share a small house with Jenny. He would go from being one of many breadwinners to being the sole breadwinner and would be responsible for providing for Jenny and any children she bore. Instead of giving his wages to his mother, he'd give them to his wife for housekeeping, and Jenny would do everything for him—cooking, cleaning and caring for him. In return, John would have a friend by his side for the rest of his life and a lover in his bed. He would never be lonely again.

Looking at Dorothy, Edward felt desolate, knowing that he could never be her husband and lover, and as much as he dreamed about it, he would never experience the pleasure of lying with her.

After the service, the bride and groom walked down the aisle. The massive grins on their faces told Edward what he wanted to know. They were delighted to be married.

The bridesmaids followed them out of the church, and then the congregation stood up and left.

Outside, Edward felt a hand on his arm.

'You'll come back to our place, won't you, Ed?' asked Mrs Robson. 'We're havin' a bit of a do for them.'

'I'd love to Mrs Robson. Thank you!'

He retrieved his horse from the boy, and the boy's face lit up when Edward gave him another halfpenny for his trouble.

'Thank you, mister. Thank you!'

'You're welcome, young man. You've earned it. You've done a good job of looking after Brandy.'

He mounted his horse and rode to Rookhope alongside the Robson family and their friends in a convoy of horses and carts.

Mrs Robson and her daughters had prepared a magnificent spread, and Edward tucked into the food and the ale, which flowed freely for the rest of the afternoon and into the evening. People stood and chatted in the kitchen, the parlour, and outside in the farmyard.

At dusk, Mr Robson lit candles outside. Mr Patterson from the village picked up his fiddle and played lively folk music, and the guests danced, spinning and twirling around the farmyard.

His inhibitions lowered, Edward asked Dorothy to dance, and when she nodded, they joined in. He loved holding her in his arms and watching her smile and laugh. Her body was warm and welcoming, and he held her close, reluctant to let her go.

When the music finished, she smiled up at him and, holding hands, led him around the side of the barn, where she put her arms around his waist and looked up at him, her lips waiting for his kiss.

Edward may have behaved differently if he had been sober, but he lowered his lips to meet hers, and they kissed gently at first and then more deeply. His hands moved over her slim waist and around to the curves of her bottom.

Dorothy pulled out his shirt and moved her hands beneath it, caressing his skin.

He kissed her ear and neck, then his lips moved down over

her collarbone towards her cleavage, his hands on her breasts, gently squeezing them.

'So, that's where you've got to,' said John.

The couple jumped apart at the sound of his voice. Edward tucked in his shirt and hoped John couldn't see well in the dark.

'Mother's lookin' for you, Dot. You'd better go inside.'

'Shall we have another drink?' asked Edward after Dorothy left them.

'I think you've had enough for one night, Ed. Maybe you should sleep it off in the barn.' In a low voice, he added, 'Dot's me sister and she thinks a lot about you. You'd better not do anythin' to hurt her.'

'I would never hurt her, John. I promise. I love her.'

'Well, mebbe you'd better step up and ask her to marry you, rather than fumbling around with her outside in the dark.'

John left and returned to the party, leaving Edward alone. He wandered into the barn, where he lay down on the hay and smiled. In his drunken, besotted state, he thought there was a possibility that he might just do that.

The following morning, Edward woke with a start. There were voices in the farmyard, and they seemed louder than usual. He put his hands to his head and remembered that he'd drank a lot of ale the day before, and then, he remembered what had happened with Dorothy after they had danced, and he shook his head, feeling ashamed that he had not been able to control himself in her arms. He was pleased that John had intervened when he had and stopped him from doing something he would no doubt have regretted.

The pleasure and passion he had felt when he was with Dorothy far surpassed anything he had experienced before, and the knowledge that he could never take her as his wife was like a knife to his heart.

He got up and went to the well, where he splashed water over his face, and then went into the kitchen.

Mrs Robson had made eggs, bacon, and bread for breakfast. Although Edward felt a little queasy, he sat at the table and ate the food.

Dorothy entered the room and blushed wildly when she saw Edward, his shirt open at the neck and his hair loose around his face.

'Have you eaten yet?' he asked.

'No, I get mine when everyone else has finished, and then I clear up.'

'Can we go for a walk after you've done that?' asked Edward.

'It's Sunday,' said Mrs Robson. 'She's goin' to church with us this mornin'.'

Edward's face fell as he realised he wouldn't see Dorothy alone before he went home. He had to leave by noon to return before nightfall. Highwaymen were out after dark, and he didn't want to run into trouble. He couldn't go later and stay in lodgings for the night either, as he wouldn't get back to Silksworth in time for work the next day. He had no choice but to leave without speaking to her in private, and after the events of the previous night, he really wished he could do that.

Accepting it wouldn't happen, he bade her farewell in the kitchen, taking her hand and kissing her cheek. Mrs Robson pretended not to notice, but he saw the smile on her face.

'Goodbye, Ed. I hope we'll see you again soon,' said Mrs Robson as he left the house.

He sought out John before he left and found him fixing the byre door.

'What happened here?' asked Edward, looking at the splintered wood.

'A heifer kicked the door down this mornin'. Father took a newborn calf off her to check it over in the daylight, and she went berserk. She kicked the door in, and it shattered, as you can see, and she barged through it to get to her calf. Father was lucky she didn't go for him. Them horns could have done him some damage.

'Do you want a hand fixing it?'

'I'm nearly done, but thanks.'

'When are you moving to Nenthead?' asked Edward.

'The house will be vacant from Saturday, so we'll be takin' our stuff over at the weekend. Why? Do you have somethin' for me?'

'Yes. I'll let you get settled and I'll come over in a month or so.'

Edward said farewell to his friend and went to the field for his horse, keeping watch for a wild heifer with a young calf at foot.

Chapter 26

Edward was eager to return to Nenthead. He had delivered a batch of silver to John before Christmas, but he'd had to wait months for the snow to clear before he could venture over the hills to collect the melted-down silver.

Edward dismounted outside the solitary cottage, secured his horse in the small garth behind the house and knocked at the door.

'Come in,' said Jenny. 'John's just havin' his tea. It's mutton broth and bread tonight. Will you have some?'

'Yes, please, Jenny,' he said. 'That's very kind of you. You're lookin' well.'

Jenny blushed, thanked him under her breath, and then went into the kitchen to bring him some food.

'She's expectin',' said John, beaming. 'That's why she's lookin' so well.'

'Congratulations!'

Jenny returned with a bowl of broth and a plate of bread and placed them on the table. 'Sit down and eat it before it gets cold,' she said.

142

Edward sat down. 'John's just told us your news. You must be so pleased.'

Jenny and John grinned at each other, and she said, 'Aye, we are.'

As he ate heartily, Edward realised he was jealous of his friend. John was settled here in a cosy cottage with a woman he loved, and they had a child on the way. As if that wasn't enough, he had a good job and decent prospects at the smelt mill. Sometimes, he wondered if he'd made the right choice to spend his life acquiring money to help a few children.

But then he remembered the boys and girls who had lived in the orphanage with him, boys and girls who had no benefactor to save them from the hard labour they'd had to endure from an early age or to provide them with an education and the means to better themselves. Whenever he thought about the orphanage, he pictured Mary Jane sitting on the chair looking up into the sky and then her body wrapped in a white shroud being lowered into the ground. He was doing exactly what he needed to do, he told himself.

After they finished their meal, John took Edward upstairs into the bedroom and lifted the quilt off the unused crib, uncovering a bar of gleaming silver.

Edward's face lit up when he saw it. 'It looks fantastic!' he said, picking it up to examine it more closely. 'Nobody could ever connect this to the candelabra and snuff boxes I brought over. You've done a great job.'

'I nearly got caught doin' it, mind you,' said John. 'Mr Beattie came back to the mill because he saw smoke comin' from the chimney and thought there might be a fire. I told him I was tryin' a new method of separatin' silver from the ore and that I'd let him know if it was any good. Luckily, he took me at me word and didn't come any closer to see what I was doin'.'

'He must trust you,' said Edward. 'That's good.'

'Aye, I think he does. I'm gettin' on well there. I think the company might have me in mind for management.'

'Even better!' Envious or not, Edward was pleased that his friend was doing so well.

When he left John and Jenny's cottage the following morning, John said, 'Would you mind goin' back by Rookhope? I know it's a bit out of your way, but I'll settle better knowin' that you've checked on me folks after the winter we've had.'

'Of course, I will,' said Edward. 'It'll be good to see them again.'

'Thanks.' John handed Edward the silver bar, saying, 'And keep this out of sight. I don't want me father askin' questions.'

Edward nodded to John, packed the silver in a saddle bag, thanked Jenny for her hospitality and set off home. Taking the track over to Allenheads, he rode over the hill into the valley of Rookhope.

Although he'd left Rookhope as a boy, it still felt like home. It was where he and John had played as children, roaming the moors and exploring every nook and cranny in the landscape. He knew the place well.

When he arrived at White Hall Farm, Robert, one of John's brothers, greeted him.'

'Mother and Father will be pleased to see you,' said Robert. 'They haven't had many visitors lately with the snow.'

Robert led the way into the farmhouse and shouted, 'You'll never guess who's here!'

Turning back to Edward, he said, 'Me mother's goin' deaf. You'll have to shout up.'

Mrs Robson came to the door and invited him in, fussed

around him as usual, and brought out a fruit cake, cut him a slice and made a fresh pot of tea.

Mr Robson sat by the fire smoking his pipe, a collie dog curled up by his feet. He looked up and nodded.

'I've been to see John and Jenny,' said Edward loudly, 'They're both very well.'

Mrs Robson nodded and said, 'We haven't set eyes on them since they moved over there. I think they've forgotten where we live.'

'John said to tell you they couldn't come because of the snow. It was John who asked me to come over this way to see that—'

Edward stopped mid-sentence when Dorothy entered the kitchen. It was six months since he'd seen her, and he'd forgotten how beautiful she was.

'Dorothy,' he said. 'It's good to see you.'

She smiled at him awkwardly as she passed and opened the front door to step outside.

'Please, excuse me,' he said to her parents, and when he moved towards the door, he saw a look pass between them. They thought he'd come all this way to see their daughter, but that wasn't his intention.

Could it have been John's?

In the yard, Dorothy smiled cheekily at Edward and asked, 'Are you followin' me?'

'I suppose I am,' he replied. He knew he should avoid being alone with her because she might misconstrue his intentions, but he couldn't stay away from her whenever she was near him. It was as if there was an invisible thread pulling him towards her.

'Do you think you'll move back to Rookhope?' she asked unexpectedly.

Edward thought about her question. He had a decent job in Silksworth. There were several solicitors in the dale, and he could probably get a job clerking for one of them if he wanted to, but his ambition in life was to see the orphans in Sunderland well cared for, and maybe children in other towns too, if he could raise enough funds.

Could I leave them behind and return home?

'I don't know,' he said honestly. 'Perhaps sometime in the future.'

Looking slightly disappointed by his response, she asked, 'What's it like where you live?'

Realising that Dorothy had travelled no further than Durham and Hexham, he admired her interest in discovering more about other places. They sat on a wooden bench at the edge of the yard, and he told her about where he worked, the cottage in the woods that he shared with Tommy, and the town of Sunderland.

She appeared to drink in every word, imagining the places he spoke of. He had no idea she was picturing herself living in that cottage as his wife, walking through the woods with him, hand in hand, shopping in the town, and loving him at night in the tiny house. It never crossed his mind because there was no place in his life for a wife.

Dorothy reached out her hand, placed it in Edward's and looked up into his eyes.

'Edward, we like each other, don't we?' she asked.

'Of course, we do. We always have. Why did you ask that?'

Taking him by surprise, she leaned over and kissed his lips. He reacted instinctively, taking her into his arms and returning the kiss.

They were interrupted by the latch on the house door, and

their lips parted reluctantly.

'Don't mind me,' said Robert as he walked past, smirking.

Edward looked into Dorothy's eyes. He didn't doubt her feelings for him or his for her, but he couldn't take their relationship any further and he released her from his embrace.

'I suppose I'd better be going.'

'Aye,' she said. 'I didn't expect you'd be stayin' long. You've got a long ride ahead of you.'

Rising from the seat, he looked down into Dorothy's face. Her blue eyes were focused on him, her pupils dilated, her pink lips slightly parted. He wanted to sit by her side and kiss her again, but with a gigantic effort, he kissed her cheek instead and turned back towards the house, where he went into the kitchen to say farewell to the family.

Dorothy hadn't moved from the seat when he came out, and she watched him mount his horse and ride out of the farmyard. As he turned to wave, he thought he saw tears in her eyes.

John's words came back to him. Despite his promise to his friend, Edward knew he'd hurt Dorothy by leaving her again without speaking about their future.

Chapter 27

Edward and Tommy had been stealing from large houses in Sunderland, Durham, and everywhere in between for two years and in that time, they had become accomplished house-breakers and more ambitious, too. With the horses, they could travel further from the cottage, and their new outlet for silver allowed them to handle greater quantities.

It was ironic, thought Edward, that it had been his father's attitude and lavish lifestyle that had made him want to make money in the first place, and now, he was outside his father's house with that single intention.

Granby House had always been Edward's ultimate goal. On the surface, he wanted to redistribute a little of his father's wealth to a worthy cause, but underneath, there was a need for vengeance, and he hoped this act of rebellion might help to heal the hurt that Lord Malham had caused him in the past. Lord Malham had so much money that losing a few pieces of silver would mean nothing to him, Edward suspected, and wondered if he'd even notice that they had gone.

The mansion house was in complete darkness apart from a

148

single light glowing in a window of the servants' wing. Edward and Tommy hid in the shrubbery at the edge of the front lawn, watching and waiting. They had seen nobody since they'd arrived almost an hour earlier.

'It's odd that there's nobody about,' said Edward. 'Perhaps Lord Malham is away.'

'That's good if he is,' said Tommy. 'If some of the servants have gone with him, there won't be as many people here to see us.'

They circled the house, looking in the windows to see where the silver was kept. They spotted a small room next to the butler's office lined with shelves, and the shelves contained large pieces of silver such as vases, trays and candlesticks. There was a cupboard across one wall, which they suspected would contain cutlery and smaller items.

Tommy used a crowbar to lift the sash window. There was a loud crack when the lock broke away from the wood, and the men waited in silence to see if it had disturbed anyone. After a minute or so, confident that they hadn't been heard, Tommy helped Edward to climb through the window, and Edward began to gather items from the shelves and pass them through the window to Tommy outside.

'That's enough,' Tommy whispered. 'We can't carry any more.'

Edward didn't listen. He intended to take as much of Lord Malham's property as possible, thinking they'd hide what they couldn't carry and return another time to retrieve it.

Working quickly and quietly, he continued to pass the silver to his friend, who piled it up by the wall.

Eventually, Edward climbed out and looked astonished by how many items were there, gleaming in the moonlight.

'We'll take what we can and leave the rest behind the bushes near the gates. We can come back for it another night.'

They filled the two hessian sacks they'd brought with them with the smaller pieces, slung them over their shoulders, and carried some larger pieces in their arms. They reached the gates, deposited their stash in the bushes as planned, and returned to the pile they had left by the window. They had no more sacks, so they placed the smaller items in their pockets, carried the rest, and walked briskly towards the gates.

A loud whistle startled them, and they looked around for where the sound had come from, but they couldn't see anything in the darkness. They heard dogs barking, a lot of dogs, and the sound was getting louder.

Still carrying the silver, they ran across the lawn towards the gates, but the dogs were getting nearer and nearer. Edward dropped everything he was carrying and sprinted to the gates. Tommy held on to his silver and tried to reach the gates, but the hounds were close—very close. Edward grabbed Tommy's arm and tried to pull his friend through the gates and close them before the dogs could catch him, but a mean-looking hound leapt through the air and grabbed Tommy's hand with its mouth, and Edward heard the crunch of bones a split second before Tommy's scream. The silver pieces Tommy had been holding clattered loudly as they hit the ground.

Edward kicked the dog hard, and it yelped, releasing Tommy's hand from its jaws, and then he slammed the gate shut.

As they ran across the fields to where they had hidden their horses, Tommy held his injured hand against his chest, dripping blood along the way.

Edward took off his scarf and wrapped it around Tommy's

hand, tying it tightly, and then he lifted Tommy onto his horse and said, 'Can you ride?'

'Aye,' said Tommy, picking up the reins in one hand. 'She'll follow Brandy.'

In the distance, they could hear the foxhounds baying at the gates, wanting to give chase.

Edward didn't waste another second. He kicked his mare into a gallop and sped away, checking that Tommy was following. As they rode home, he realised that this was the first time either of them had been injured, and it was the closest they had come to being caught. If the hounds had been released from the grounds, they would have followed their trail, caught up to them within minutes, and torn them and their horses to pieces.

Thank God they had escaped.

Tommy slid down his mare's side at the cottage and wobbled when his feet touched the ground. Edward put his arm around his friend, noticing he was shaking, and helped him inside. He sat Tommy at the table and lit a candle.

Edward took a blanket off Tommy's bed and wrapped it around his friend's shoulders, then slowly removed the scarf from Tommy's hand and grimaced at what he saw—a mangled mixture of blood, flesh and bone.

'I can't do anything for this, Tommy. I'll have to get the doctor.'

'What will we tell him?'

'That you got mauled by a wild dog in the woods. No witnesses. You blacked out. Found your way home and woke me.'

'Aye, alright.'

'We don't have any liquor in the house,' said Edward, placing his hand on Tommy's shoulder. 'I'll bring some back with me—I promise.'

Realising he still had a few pieces of silver in his pockets, he emptied them onto the table and emptied Tommy's pockets, too, and then he hid everything in the stable before setting off for Silksworth.

Half an hour later, he returned with Doctor Page, and they entered the cottage to find Tommy still seated at the table, crying with the pain, a pool of congealed blood on the table beneath his hand.

Edward poured a glass of whisky from the bottle the doctor had kindly given him and passed it to Tommy, who gulped it down.

'Mr Earle has told me what happened, Tommy. Now, let's have a look at you,' said the doctor. 'I need more light in here. Do you have any more candles?'

Edward lit a couple of tallow candles and placed them on the table.

'That's better.'

The doctor lifted Tommy's hand, causing Tommy to wince, and as the doctor carried out his examination, Edward refilled Tommy's glass.

'It's not good, I'm afraid,' said Doctor Page. 'The bones in the hand are broken in many places. The muscles are severely lacerated. The tenons, too. Open wound. Infection. Rabies possibly.'

Edward thought it sounded like the doctor was working through a checklist.

'Can you fix it?' he asked.

'It's too badly damaged, I'm afraid,' said the doctor, shaking his head. 'There's only one solution for it.'

Edward and Tommy both looked at him.

'Amputation,' he said.

Edward's eyes widened in horror, and Tommy began to wail loudly.

'We can do it here, now, or you can bring him to the surgery in the morning.'

Edward thought he might faint and sat down in the armchair.

'On second thoughts,' said the doctor, 'tomorrow would be better as I'll be able to see what I'm doing in daylight. Let him drink the rest of that bottle. It'll help with the pain tonight and I'll have another one waiting for him at the surgery in the morning.'

Lapsing into his old dialect, Edward said, 'Aye, I'll fetch him ower in the mornin'.'

'I noticed that your roof is leaking,' said the doctor, looking at a bucket in the middle of the floor. 'You should get it fixed. Damp houses are not good for one's health.'

'We'll see to it,' said Edward, knowing that he couldn't afford to hire a thatcher to fix the roof on his wages, and the money they made from house-breaking would never be used for anything other than the children.

When the doctor had left, Edward filled Tommy's glass again and held his friend as he sobbed. It was his fault Tommy had been injured, and as a result, he was going to lose his hand. He wouldn't be able to cut wood for the estate anymore.

What could he do with only one hand?

Edward's face was wet with tears, too.

The following day, Edward sat a drunken Tommy on Ghost, mounted his horse, and held Tommy's reins.

'Hold onto her mane with your good hand, nice and tight,'

said Edward. 'Don't let go.'

They rode to Silksworth, Tommy singing a few lewd songs he'd learnt from the sailors on the way, still intoxicated from the whisky he'd had during the night. When they reached the village, Tommy was leaning over the horse's neck, his head resting on her mane, and his arms dangling down.

They stopped outside the doctor's surgery, and Edward tethered the horses, helped Tommy down and walked him into the doctor's house.

'You can stay if you wish,' offered Dr Page, 'or return for him in an an hour or two.'

Edward could not watch his friend having his hand removed. Just the thought of it made his stomach churn. He wanted to go to an inn and have a drink, but once he started, he knew he wouldn't stop, and he needed to stay sober to get Tommy home after the surgery.

Instead, he walked around the village and tried to calm his breathing. It was Sunday, and everyone seemed to be heading to church. Edward considered attending the service to pray for Tommy, and the thought made him chuckle. Since Mr Kelly and the vicar had indoctrinated him, he hated religion with a vengeance. It would be hypocritical for him to ask for God's help now.

He saw Mr and Mrs Travis leave their house and walked over to speak with them.

'Edward, whatever has happened? You look dreadful,' said Mr Travis.

'A friend has had an accident. He's with Doctor Page now having his hand amputated. I hope you can manage without me in the office this week. I'd like to stay with him until his condition improves.'

'By all means, Edward. You're due some time off. I'll expect you back a week tomorrow.'

'Thank you, Mr Travis,' said Edward. 'I appreciate that.'

'Take good care of yourself, too,' added Mrs Travis. 'You look like you've had a dreadful shock.'

Chapter 28

Hawthorn Cottage, Silksworth
September 1769

Tommy's wound took weeks to heal, but the impact of his injury would last a lifetime. Edward couldn't imagine how his friend would manage with only one hand, and he grimaced whenever he saw Tommy trying to do everyday tasks, from washing himself to making food. Everything was a struggle for him.

Edward blamed himself for what had happened that night and hated himself for putting Tommy in harm's way. He wondered why Tommy hadn't dropped the silver and sprinted to the gates when he'd heard the hounds as he had, but even as he asked himself the question, he knew the answer—Tommy had wanted to return with as much silver as he could—to please him.

He knew his next instalment at the orphanage was due and wondered if he could continue paying regular contributions. The orphans had benefited so much from his money. On his last visit, he learned that a tutor had been employed two mornings a week to teach the younger children their letters and that they had been taken to the beach at Roker and paddled in the sea. He smiled to himself.

How much better was that than working in a pin factory?

One thing was for sure—he and Tommy couldn't steal from large houses anymore to make money. He couldn't pass valuables outside to a man with only one hand, and Tommy could only carry half of what he could before.

Can I do it alone?

He doubted that very much. He and Tommy had always worked as a team.

Edward considered the wages he received from his office job. It was a reasonable salary, but the few pennies left over at the end of the week wouldn't go far towards the food, clothing, and basic education he provided for the orphans.

How would they fare without his money?

Their education would be stopped, and the children would be sent out to work again from a younger age, their earnings used for their upkeep, as they had done before he'd stepped in to help. The situation was dire. Edward put his head in his hands.

'What are you thinkin' about?' asked Tommy, seated by the fire, his arm raised across his chest, showing the scarred stump where his hand should have been.

'The children,' said Edward sadly. 'How can we help them now?'

'Aye, I thought that might be what was troublin' you. I've been thinkin' about that an' all, and I think I've come up with the answer. It's riskier than what we've been doin', but it might work.'

Interested to hear what his friend had to say, Edward leaned forward in his chair and asked, 'And what's that?'

'We could be highwaymen.'

They were both silent for a moment while Tommy's words sank in, and Edward contemplated the implications of robbing travellers on the highways rather than house-breaking.

Yes, they could be highwaymen. They had horses, and Tommy could still ride despite losing his hand. They would need to acquire a pair of pistols, but that shouldn't be too difficult; he'd seen many firearms when burgling large houses but had never thought to take them.

With highway robbery, there was less chance of being caught than stealing from houses, as they could leave the scene of the crime more rapidly, but if they were caught, the consequences were much more severe. Thieves were imprisoned or sent to the colonies; highwaymen were hanged.

Stealing from coaches travelling on the toll roads would give them the means to continue funding the orphanage, which was the most crucial factor in Edward's decision.

'Yes, it could work,' said Edward tentatively. 'We would only take from travellers that appear wealthy. I won't steal from the poor.'

'Agreed,' said Tommy, 'We know what it's like to have nothin'.'

'We'd have to wear a disguise of some sort, so the victims couldn't give an accurate description of us.'

Tommy held up his handless arm in despair. 'But how can I disguise this?'

'We'll get a prosthetic hand made for you—a wooden one. With a glove over it, it won't be obvious that it's not a real hand.'

'You think of everythin', you do, Edward. That's a great idea. It might help with the lasses an' all. They mightn't be as scared of me if I have a wooden hand.'

Edward smiled. He was pleased Tommy had perked up and was thinking about girls again. That meant he was ready to go out and face the world.

'Would you like to go to the inn tonight and have a drink to celebrate?' asked Edward. 'I'll pay.'

'Aye, why not? It's ages since we've been out for a pint.'

Chapter 29

Sunderland Town
October 1769

Edward went into town to collect the two outfits he'd ordered, clothing he considered suitable for highwaymen, one set for Tommy and one for himself. He had decided it would be safer for them if they wore a completely different set of clothes just for going out onto the roads at night, quite different from the clothing they usually wore, so if anyone described the men who had robbed them, nobody would recognise the clothes as theirs.

He had ordered the coats, shirts, waistcoats and breeches at several different shops, so the tailors, if questioned, couldn't identify the man or men the police were looking for. He collected the items from the shops and walked briskly up the street, eager to get them to the cottage and hide them.

Whenever Edward visited Sunderland, he wore his gentleman's clothing in case anyone from the orphanage saw him. However, he had not expected to meet Mr Travis and his wife there.

'Edward Earle, you are looking dandy! I love your coat,' said Mrs Travis, feeling the quality of the cloth at his sleeve.

'Thank you.' He said, feeling ill at ease under their inspection. The clothes he wore in the office were decent, but the ones he wore in town were grander and much more expensive. 'I like to dress well when I visit the tailors,' he said, holding up the boxes and revealing the name of the last tailor's shop he had visited. 'You get much better service if they think you have money to spend.'

Mr Travis laughed. 'I'm sure you're right, Edward. I must remember that the next time I need a new suit.'

'Edward!' Charlotte Liddell waved at him from across the street, and then, carrying at least four boxes, she stumbled over to him and smiled sweetly at the couple she'd seen him talking to.

Mr and Mrs Travis looked at Edward, silently asking for an introduction.

Edward had never envisaged that his two worlds would collide like this. His heart beating wildly, he made the introductions.

'Mr and Mrs Travis from Silksworth, I'm pleased to introduce you to Miss Charlotte Liddell from Sunderland.'

'Edward, would you be a darling and take these boxes for me?'

Charlotte dumped her boxes on top of the ones Edward already had in his arms.

'I'm very glad to make your acquaintance, Mr Travis, Mrs Travis,' she said, holding out her gloved hand to Mr Travis, who appeared delighted to kiss it.

'Come on, Mr Travis, we have a lot to do today,' said his wife. 'We'll leave the young couple to their shopping.'

Mr Travis winked at Edward as he turned to leave.

Edward's body was covered in cold sweat, and his mind

worked overtime.

Will my employer meet Miss Liddell socially?

Edward doubted it, but if they did meet again, his name would undoubtedly be a topic of conversation. He was relieved he'd given his real name at the orphanage, so at least everyone knew him as Edward.

What will Charlotte think if she discovers I'm a lowly solicitor's clerk and not the gentleman she believes me to be?

He hoped she would never find out.

'Edward, you're miles away. You haven't heard a word I've said, have you?' asked Charlotte. 'I asked if you'd like to come to the horse races at Newcastle with me next weekend. Everybody will be there. Please say you'll come.'

'I'm very sorry, Charlotte, but I'm afraid I must decline. I have arranged to visit friends next weekend. Perhaps another time.'

Charlotte pouted at his refusal but continued to chat about everyone she had seen since their last encounter. It was as though she expected he knew the people she mentioned, but in reality, they moved in very different social circles.

Chapter 30

Edward and Tommy dressed in their new outfits, comprised of long coats with deep pockets, knee-high black boots, large cocked hats and scarves to hide their faces, all in dark colours so they would blend into the darkness and shadows of night.

Tommy fastened his new wooden hand onto his arm and then put on his gloves. The fingers of the hand could be positioned to grip things, and it looked just like a real hand with the glove on, as Edward had said it would.

Tommy had practised riding Ghost, holding the reins in the prosthetic hand, which freed his good hand to take things from their victims, hold Edward's horse, or wield a knife or pistol.

'This hand would make a good weapon, don't you think?' asked Tommy, thumping the table with it. 'Imagine gettin' hit with a wooden fist. It would do some damage.'

'Yes, I'm sure it would. Just make sure it's not me or yourself that you hit with it!' replied Edward with a laugh.

'Don't highwaymen have nicknames?' asked Tommy. 'I could be *The Wooden Hand* or *The Wooden Fist.*'

'That's not a good idea if you want to disguise the fact that you have a wooden hand!' Edward laughed loudly.

'Damn it!' said Tommy. 'I'll have to think of another name now. Seriously though, are you sure we should be doin' this?'

'As sure as I'll ever be. We're both accomplished riders so we should have no difficulty escaping after the deed is done.'

'Don't start usin' your long words on me, Edward. They don't impress me,' said Tommy. 'What the heck does accomplished mean, anyway?'

'It means that we both ride well.'

'Well, why didn't you just say that?' Tommy pulled anxiously at the unfamiliar clothes.

Edward checked the loaded pistol and carefully placed it in his coat pocket. Noticing that Tommy's eyes had grown wide at the site of the weapon, he said, 'It'll be alright, Tommy. It's just to threaten people into giving us their valuables. I'll not fire it.'

'So why is it loaded if you're not goin' to fire it?'

'It's loaded in case we get into trouble. Firing a shot might help us escape.'

'And what if we get caught?' asked Tommy.

'We won't get caught. Remember what I told you? We must never, ever get caught. If we think the risks are too high, we won't go through with it. Agreed?'

Tommy nodded in assent.

The men went out to the horses that were already saddled. They mounted and set off for the toll road that linked Sunderland and Durham. As the horses made their way through the woods and open fields, Edward's eyes adjusted to the darkness, and he could see reasonably well. When they reached a section of the road with trees on both sides, they stopped and waited in the shadows, dappled by the moonlight shining through the branches.

They didn't have long to wait until a beautiful carriage came by, with candle lamps on each side, highlighting the ornate gilt decoration on the doors.

Edward urged Brandy forward until they were in the middle of the road, but she wouldn't stand still when a team of horses was heading towards her at speed. Edward struggled to control her, and she turned quickly on the spot. Luckily, he managed to keep his seat. His heart raced as the horse fought him, and for the first time, Edward questioned if their mission would be successful.

Tommy moved Ghost over to them, and she stood by Brandy's side, calming the younger horse.

The carriage slowed and then stopped in front of the highwaymen. One of the two carriage horses neighed loudly, its breath clouding in the cold air. The coachman looking down at them was pale.

Edward was unsure if it was fear or the moonlight that drained him of colour. He rode to the side of the carriage and recognised the crest on the door as belonging to the Balliols, one of the wealthiest families in the region. Edward knocked on the window, and a gentleman inside opened the door.

'Not again!' he exclaimed, unable to contain his annoyance. 'This is the second time I've been stopped on this road this year. Please, show me some mercy!'

Edward saw that the man wore a gold watch chain, which probably meant he had a gold fob watch tucked away in his pocket. Looking over to the lady sitting by the gentlemen's side, he admired the necklace adorning her slim neck and the matching pendulous earrings. The clear stones sparkled in the low light; they had to be diamonds. The set must be worth a small fortune, thought Edward.

'Please, sir, I'd be grateful if you'd give me your watch and your lady's necklace and earrings,' Edward said politely.

'And if I don't want to give them to you?' asked the gentleman haughtily.

Edward took the pistol from his coat pocket and pointed it towards the open door.

The gentleman quickly unclasped his wife's necklace while she pulled off her earrings and passed them to Edward, and then he removed the watch from his pocket.

Edward returned the firearm to his pocket and thanked the couple, bowing theatrically to them before he and Tommy disappeared into the woods.

As he rode away, Edward couldn't believe how easy the whole process had been, and the items they'd recovered were exquisite. Far better than anything he'd ever taken from a house. Blood rushed through his veins, he felt elated, and as soon as they'd ridden a reasonable distance from the road, he whooped with joy.

Tommy laughed loudly.

They slowed their horses to a walk as they entered the woods surrounding their cottage.

'It worked,' said Tommy. 'How easy was that?'

'I think we've found our calling!' said Edward triumphantly, stopping his horse in the clearing. 'I'll tether the horses and we should get changed out of these clothes quickly. We don't want anyone seeing us dressed like this.'

Chapter 31

The Road from Sunderland to Gateshead
December 1769

Edward and Tommy hid in the woods at the edge of the road, sitting silently on their horses in the darkness, listening for travellers. As they waited patiently, they heard the leafless branches swaying against each other in the breeze, a pair of owls hooting, and the howl of a fox seeking a mate.

It had been a quiet evening. Only a lowly farmer had used the road within the last hour, and Edward and Tommy had stayed hidden in the shadows, letting him pass unheeded.

Eventually, the sound of hooves, the rattle of a harness and the wheels of a carriage on the road could be heard. That is what they had been waiting for. Their hearts pounded, and excitement filled the air.

'Just one horse,' whispered Edward. 'It might not be worth stopping.'

'Aw, come on,' said Tommy. 'We've been hangin' around here for ages. This might be our only chance tonight. Do you want to go home empty-handed?'

Edward did not want to go home empty-handed.

'Alright. Do you have your gloves on?'

'Aye, I have, Mother,' replied Tommy sarcastically. 'And me scarf pulled up to hide me ugly mug.'

Edward rolled his eyes and said, 'Let's go.'

The men urged their horses out of the cover of the trees and onto the verge. They saw a horse and carriage travelling on the rutted track in the moonlight. Edward pulled up his scarf to hide the lower half of his face and pulled down his hat so his eyes were in shadow, and then he rode into the middle of the road and faced the approaching vehicle.

The startled carriage horse neighed loudly as it was brought to an abrupt halt.

A man called out from the carriage, 'Why have we stopped? We're in the middle of nowhere.'

'Sorry, sir,' replied the coachman, looking at Edward, his eyes full of fear.

Edward nodded reassuringly at the driver. 'Don't try anything and you won't be harmed.'

With his hand on the pistol in his coat pocket, Edward shouted, 'Step out of the carriage and deliver your purse.'

'What's the meanin' of this?' The passenger opened the door and stepped out onto the road. 'I have nae got any money on me.' He held out his purse and tipped it upside down—the bag was empty.

Edward instantly recognised the man as Mr Dunsmore from the orphanage, and his heart pounded faster in his chest.

Will Mr Dunsmore recognise me?

His first instinct was to flee before his identity was discovered, but he couldn't disappoint Tommy or let down the poor children.

In a broad northern accent, Edward said to Tommy, 'Hold me horse an' I'll search the carriage.'

Tommy moved forward and took Brandy's reins. Edward jumped down, passing within inches of Mr Dunsmore, and opened the door to peer inside the carriage. In the murky darkness, he was shocked to see a woman cowering against the opposite door.

'Are you wearin' jewellery?' he asked.

The woman remained silent, shaking with fear; her face turned away from him.

Edward touched her arm gently and said, 'I won't hurt you, but if you have a necklace, a ring or a brooch, I'll take it, please.'

Slowly, the woman turned towards him, and he saw she was Sarah from the orphanage. He wished he had fled the scene as his instincts had told him to do. He was sure Sarah would know who he was, even in the low light and with him using his old Weardale accent. Now, he really was in trouble.

'I don't have any jewellery,' she said, drawing her eyebrows together as though she was trying to fathom out who he was. He noticed she had stopped shaking, too; she no longer feared him. He was very concerned that she had recognised him.

Edward nodded and left her alone. Returning to Mr Dunsmore, he kept his head down and his face obscured.

'If you're carryin' a purse, there must be some money somewhere. Have you hidden it?'

Edward noticed Mr Dunsmore flinch and briefly look towards the carriage floor. Edward returned to the carriage and lifted the mat on the floor, under which he found some coins hidden, a couple of crowns bearing the head of good King George and a few shillings and pennies.

'Thank you for these,' said Edward, putting the coins in his pocket. 'I'll take your coat and buckles, and then you can go.'

'But it's freezin' the night.'

Removing the pistol from his pocket, Edward repeated his words.

Mr Dunsmore hurriedly removed the gilt buckles from his shoes, handed them to Edward, and then removed his coat.

'Can we go now?' asked the Scotsman, already shivering in the cold night air.

'Aye, and thank you very much for your co-operation.'

Edward mounted his horse and galloped up the road. He could hear the hooves of Tommy's horse close behind him, and they kept galloping for several miles until they were well away from the road. Then, they slowed to a walk and entered the narrow trail into the woods, which would take them back to the safety of their cottage.

Chapter 32

Edward had a restless week, worrying whether or not Sarah had recognised him the night he'd held up their carriage on the highway, but he thought that, in all probability, she had.

When the time came for his next visit to the orphanage to make a gift of money, he hoped that his assumption was wrong, but either way, he was anxious to find out.

On his arrival, Sarah opened the door as usual, but this time, she smiled brightly at him and had a twinkle in her eye.

So, I was right. She did recognise me. Do I have a problem, or can I rely on her silence?

Mr Dunsmore must have reported the incident to the police, and he and Sarah would both have been questioned as witnesses.

Surely, if she intended to give me up, she would have done so already?

Edward thought he could trust her to keep his secret because she obviously hadn't said anything until now, but he needed to know for sure.

'Sarah, it's lovely to see you again,' he said.

'And you too, your Lordship.'

He thought he detected a stifled smile when she said the word Lordship.

'May I speak with you alone, please? Just for a moment.'

Sarah stepped onto the footpath, leaving the door behind her slightly ajar.

'I don't have long,' she said. 'Mr Dunsmore will know if I'm away for more then a few minutes.'

'I just wanted to apologise if I frightened you the other night. That is the last thing I wanted to do.'

'When the carriage first stopped and I realised there were highwaymen outside, I was petrified. I'd heard stories of people being killed in cold blood or left with nothin', not even their clothes. But I wasn't afraid once I knew it was you. You would never be cruel.' Looking at him in admiration, she said, 'You're our very own Robin Hood, stealin' from the rich and givin' to the poor. Thank you! The bairns in here have never had it so good.'

'How do you know I give the money to the orphanage?' asked Edward, perplexed. 'It's supposed to be a secret.'

'I overheard you scolding Mr Dunsmore for tellin' his wife about you. I wondered why you came here for Christmas dinner a few years ago. Now, everything makes sense.'

Edward had been angry that day he had confronted Mr Dunsmore, but he was shocked to hear he'd raised his voice loud enough for someone outside the room to hear.

'I wish they'd been somebody like you helpin' out when I was growin' up here.'

'You're an orphan?' asked Edward in disbelief.

'Aye, I was left here when I was a baby. Mrs Kelly found me on the doorstep one mornin'. I don't remember anythin'' about me parents. The only thing I have is the shawl I was wrapped in and a note from me mother askin' them to take care of me.'

Edward realised that Sarah must have been in the orphanage at the same time he and Tommy were there, and he was surprised that they didn't know each other, but he'd had little to do with the girls after the death of Mary Jane.

'Oh, Sarah,' he said, taking her hand. 'I'm sorry you had to spend your childhood in the orphanage, but what I don't understand is why you're still here. You must be what, twenty?'

'I'm nineteen. I got placed in a big house when I was twelve and was there for a couple of years, but it didn't work out, so I came back.

'Why didn't it work out?'

Sarah lowered her eyes, and Edward noticed that she blushed slightly.

'Why did you leave the job and come back here? Tell me, please.'

'The missus took a dislike to me. She said I was too pretty for a housemaid and attracted too much attention.'

Edward raised his eyebrows.

'She didn't like me because her husband kept lookin' at me. That's why she sent me back.'

'That's hardly fair.'

'I know, but it's not that bad here, really,' said Sarah. 'I have somewhere safe to sleep and I get me meals provided.'

'And what does he pay you for your work?'

'I don't get paid. I work for my keep.'

'I don't believe it,' said Edward. 'The mean bastard. I'm sorry about the language, but he is. The man's wife comes from a very wealthy family and yet here you are, practically a slave.'

'I should be gettin' back.'

Looking Sarah in the eye, Edward asked, 'Can I count on you to keep my secret?'

'I won't tell a soul,' she said sincerely.

He kissed her cheek and said, 'Thank you.'

'How could I possibly give you up? If you get caught, it's the children who will suffer.'

Chapter 33

Edward woke as a chink of light hit his face. He blinked wildly and wiped his eyes. He sat up and saw Tommy was already awake, sitting on the stone floor.

'What are you doing down there?' asked Edward.

'Just thinkin'.'

'What about?'

'Everythin'.'

Edward had been thinking about everything since he'd been captured, too. Everything he'd done. Everything he'd said. Every person he had hurt.

'I know what we did was wrong, in a way,' said Tommy, 'but we didn't do it for us. We did it to help the bairns. What I was thinkin' is that we're not likely to get out of here—'

'But we—'

'No, Edward, let me finish what I want to say.' Tommy smiled. 'I'm alright with it. Whatever happens. If we go to court and get convicted, that's as it should be. We did steal from them houses. We did stop them carriages and take stuff

175

from the passengers. We are thieves and highwaymen, and we deserve to be punished for what we did. After yesterday, I've decided I'm not goin' to be frightened of anythin' anymore. I'll accept whatever happens.'

Edward nodded slowly. His friend had a point. They were guilty of the crimes for which they'd been arrested.

Although the house-breaking and highway robbery initially had been Tommy's idea, Edward knew he would never have gone through with either without his full backing. He held himself responsible for leading Tommy astray and putting him in harm's way, and because of him, Tommy had not only suffered in the past but was likely to be hanged soon.

He desperately wished he could return to his eighteenth birthday, the day he'd decided what he would do with his life and choose a different path with a different outcome.

'I'm sorry,' said Edward, leaning forward and putting his hand on Tommy's shoulder.

'We did good.' Tommy smiled, at peace with himself. 'I can't get that Christmas dinner out of me mind and the look on them little bairns' faces.'

Edward lay back down and looked at the cobwebbed ceiling, noticing the light reflecting off the water droplets suspended on the silken threads. He was glad Tommy had accepted the situation and seemed contented, but he didn't feel the same about what they'd done or their future.

Thinking about the lies he'd told, the people he'd deceived, and all of the dishonesty in his life, he was ashamed and wished he could make amends.

He was sorry he had hurt Charlotte. He knew from the outset that she had designs on him as a suitor, and he'd been flattered by the attention from the beautiful, wealthy young woman. He wasn't sure, but he suspected she may have had genuine feelings for him.

He had been a cad. Not only had he done nothing to deter her advances, his actions had encouraged her. He should never have gone to the tea shop or the park with her because she'd misconstrued his acceptance as a declaration of his interest. And he should never have kissed her when he was hiding from the vicar—that had been despicable. The kiss had been meaningless to him; he'd simply used her to shield his face. Throughout their acquaintance, he had been playing a game, acting the part of a wealthy, young aristocrat, but their dalliance had meant much more to her.

He had so many regrets regarding Dorothy that he didn't know where to start. His feelings for her were stronger than ever, and he knew they were returned, but for years, he had misled her with the pretence that they might someday have a future together. He'd been a coward. He should have told her years ago that they couldn't be together. Seeing Dorothy with another man would have been agonising for him, but that was the only way she could ever be married and have the family she craved. He had been so selfish—he should have let her go.

Tears ran down his face, and he wiped them away and sniffed loudly.

The one thing he didn't regret in his life, the only thing, was helping the orphans in Sunderland. Tommy was right when he said that they 'did good'. They had done a lot of good. All of their crimes had been committed with the very best of intentions.

Edward couldn't just lie there, feeling sorry for himself, believing his life was over. He wanted to live. He wanted to be free. He wanted nothing more than to spend the rest of his life with Dorothy—but even if he managed to escape from the gaol, he knew that dream could never come true.

He wanted Tommy to survive this ordeal and be safe and happy always. He had been a great friend—the best. Whether Tommy had accepted his fate or not, he didn't deserve to die this way.

Edward rolled out of bed and knelt on the stone floor. He put his hands together, and he prayed.

Chapter 34

The Sunderland to Durham Road
March 1770

As they waited on horseback at the edge of the road, obscured by trees, Tommy said, 'You know, if I could go anywhere, I'd go to France.'

'Why France?' asked Edward.

'Well, it's not that far away, so the sailors say, and the women in France are prettier than the lasses over here.'

Edward laughed. Tommy had always been gullible.

'You shouldn't listen to the sailors at the docks, Tommy. There's nobody better for spinning a yarn.'

'So, the French girls aren't prettier than English girls. Is that what you're sayin'?'

'I'm certain there are beautiful women all around the world, and that we have our fair share here in England.'

'That's good to hear,' said Tommy. 'I must have been lookin' in the wrong places.'

Edward roared with laughter.

'Shush!' said Tommy, 'Someone might hear you.'

'There isn't anyone for miles around. I've never known this road to be so quiet.'

They sat silently for a while longer, and then Edward cocked his head and asked, 'Can you hear something?'

Tommy shrugged.

'There's a carriage coming, travelling fast. Four, maybe six horses. Let's get ready.'

The two men rode onto the road to halt the carriage, with Edward leading the way.

The carriage horses saw the obstruction in the road before the driver did, and they neighed loudly as they came to a sudden stop.

'What is it?' a voice from inside the carriage shouted.

'Highwaymen, sir.'

'You know what to do,' came the reply.

'Yes, sir.'

The driver lifted a pistol from the empty seat beside him and pointed it at Edward.

'Fire, damn you!' shouted the man inside the carriage.

Seeing that his friend was in grave danger, Tommy kicked his horse hard. She rushed in front of Edward's horse and galloped to the other side of the road, but the grey mare didn't stop—she continued to run over the open land.

Edward's horse reared at the sound of the gunshot and then bolted after Ghost. Edward kept low, hanging over Brandy's neck in case the coachman fired again. The horses' hooves pounded the ground as they raced away from the coach, and after they had ridden for several miles and were out of sight of the road, they pulled up their horses under a large oak tree.

Edward exhaled sharply. 'By God! That was a lucky escape.'

He looked at Tommy, and even in the moonlight, he could see that his friend was pale, and he wondered if he might be in shock; nobody had ever drawn a pistol and fired at them before.

'Are you alright, Tommy?' asked Edward.

'He got me,' said Tommy. 'He shot me.'

Edward jumped down off his horse and ran to his friend.

'Where are you hurt?' he asked, annoyed that the gun had been pointed at him, yet once again, it was Tommy who had been injured.

Tommy pointed to his left side.

Edward reached up, unbuttoned Tommy's coat and opened it to reveal his blood-soaked breeches. Taking off his scarf, Edward pressed it against the wound and placed Tommy's hand over it.

'Hold this here, and press on as hard as you can. Don't worry about riding, I'll take your reins. We'll get this fixed, Tommy. Alright?'

Tommy nodded weakly.

Edward remounted and led Tommy's horse towards home, but he wasn't sure where they were headed. He couldn't treat a gunshot wound himself.

Who can I ask for help?

Doctor Page would have been his first choice as he'd been good with Tommy when his hand was injured, but there was no way he could explain how Tommy had come by a gunshot wound. It would be the doctor's duty to inform the police, and if anyone had reported shooting at two highwaymen that night, he and Tommy would undoubtedly be arrested. He couldn't take that risk.

Who else can I trust?

John and Jenny lived too far away. Tommy would never make the journey to Cumberland in his current state.

The Robsons at Rookhope would want to know what had

happened to Tommy, and he didn't want Dorothy to know what he was involved in.

The only other person who sprung to mind was Sarah. She knew they were highwaymen and had kept their secret, so he knew he could trust her implicitly. Perhaps she would come to the cottage and tend to Tommy's wound.

He took Tommy home, helped him into the cottage and made him comfortable on his mattress. Then, he rode as quickly as he could to Sunderland. It was about three in the morning when he knocked at the orphanage door, and he was surprised when Sarah opened it a few minutes later, wearing a silk dressing gown that had seen better days.

'Edward!' she said, her eyes wide, looking up at him astride his horse.

'Sarah, I need your help,' he said. 'Please, can you come with me?'

Sarah looked around anxiously. 'How do I explain my absence?' she asked.

On his way there, Edward had thought about that and said, 'Write a note. Tell them you received a letter from a lady claiming to be your sister and that you have gone to find out if she really is your sister.'

'That's good,' she said. 'Mr Dunsmore will believe that. Give me a minute to get dressed.'

'If there are any bandages in there, bring them with you.'

Sarah nodded and went back inside, and as good as her word, she returned promptly. She handed him the bandages, and he put them in his pocket.

He took her hand and pulled her up to sit behind the saddle.

'Hold on tight,' he said, and when he felt her arms around his waist, Edward galloped the horse back to Silksworth, hoping

Tommy would still be alive when they arrived.

When they reached the cottage, he lowered Sarah to the ground and jumped down, not bothering to untack or tether his horse, which wandered toward the water trough.

Edward opened the door, and Sarah followed him into the tiny cottage, where they found Tommy lying on his mattress, still holding Edward's scarf against the wound.

'Tommy, this is Sarah. She's come here to look after you.'

Tommy smiled weakly and said, 'Thank you, Edward. You found one of the pretty ones.'

Edward winked at him, thinking that if he could recall their conversation about women earlier, he couldn't be too badly hurt.

'You're not squeamish, are you?' Edward asked Sarah.

'Hardly. It's me that deals with all the children's cuts and scrapes at the orphanage.'

'Good. Tommy was shot tonight. He has a wound on his left side and it's bleeding quite heavily.'

'Shot!'

'Yes, he was shot.'

Sarah took a deep breath. 'We should have a look at the wound and see how bad it is. He might need the doctor.'

'We can't get the doctor. He'd ask too many questions. We need to fix this ourselves.'

Sarah didn't question him. Instead, she went to the bed and said, 'Let's have a look at what you've done.'

Edward helped Sarah remove Tommy's clothing. Tommy still held the scarf to his wound as Edward had told him to and winced with pain every time he moved.

Prising his fingers off the scarf, Sarah said, 'You need to let go of that now so I can see.'

Tommy turned his face to her and nodded like a child.

The wound was behind his hip, more on his buttock, and it was a flesh wound. The musket ball had not entered his body, but it had scraped off a large area of skin and removed some of the flesh beneath.

'Is it bad?' asked Tommy.

'I've seen worse,' said Sarah, her face impassive.

Looking over her shoulder, Edward thought that he had seen worse, too, the night that the hound had mauled Tommy's hand, and suddenly, he felt nauseous.

'What shall we do?' he asked Sarah.

'I think you should sit down,' she said, noticing his pallor.

When Edward was seated, she said, 'It's bleedin' quite a lot so the wound should be clean. I can't see any bits of fabric or anythin' stuck in it. It needs to be dressed to keep it clean and to stop the bleeding.'

Edward took the bandages from his pocket and handed them to Sarah.

'It's not deep,' she said, 'but a wound that size could take a while to heal.'

'It doesn't sound like you'll be riding that horse of yours for a while,' said Edward, trying to make light of the situation.

Tommy laughed.

'Will Sarah be stayin' here with us?' he asked.

'Aye, I can stay for a while,' she replied. 'I'll stay until you're feelin' better.'

'Good,' said Tommy, grinning at Edward.

Sarah dressed the wound, and when she'd finished, she stood up and yawned.

'You need to get some sleep,' said Edward. 'Please, take my mattress. I'll sleep in the armchair.'

Chapter 35

The Orphanage, Sunderland
August 1770

After leaving Dunsmore's office, Edward bumped into Sarah in the corridor and apologised for not looking where he was going.

'How's Tommy?' she asked.

'He's much better, although he's missing his nurse,' Edward winked at her. 'I'll tell him you were asking after him.'

'Thank you.' Sarah blushed and rushed away.

Edward had always liked Sarah, but he thought even more of her after she had cared for Tommy while he recovered from the gunshot wound. He'd noticed that she and Tommy had become close during those few weeks, and he was pleased for them. They appeared to be a good match.

Edward's mind turned to Dorothy. He hadn't seen her for such a long time and missed her terribly. Not being able to court her was the one aspect of this life he hated, but it was a sacrifice he had chosen to make. There was nobody to blame but himself. But that didn't stop him from fantasising about a life with her and dreaming of her in his arms at night.

As he opened the door to leave the building, Charlotte

Liddell walked in, her arms full of boxes.

'Edward!' she said, smiling broadly. 'Fancy meeting you here.'

'It's becoming quite a habit, Miss Liddell.'

'Are you in a hurry? Perhaps we could take a stroll in the park? It's such a lovely day.'

After turning down several offers that she'd made in the past, he thought that perhaps he should accept this one. A walk in the park was safer than going to someone's house or the races, where there was more chance he would be recognised as Edward Earle, the solicitor's clerk from Silksworth.

'I have no plans for the rest of the afternoon, and I would be delighted to take a walk in the park with you.'

'Excellent! I'll just leave these boxes with Alex for safe-keeping and we'll be on our way.'

She rushed down the corridor to the office, breezed into the room, and reappeared a few seconds later. *She certainly wasn't wasting any time.*

He held out his arm, and she smiled up at him as she placed her hand on it, and he thought again that she really was a beautiful woman.

They walked along the roadside, crossed over it and entered the park through a pair of wrought iron gates. It was a hot day, and the park was more crowded than usual, with the townsfolk making the most of the excellent weather. The path was lined with lime trees, and they walked comfortably in the shade, listening to the children playing and the birds singing.

Charlotte talked about the soirées that she had attended and the events that she had planned. Her life was so far removed from his own; he couldn't imagine having so much leisure time to fill with pointless social activities.

As they approached a wooden seat, Charlotte said, 'It's rather hot with all these layers. Perhaps we could sit for a while?'

'Certainly,' said Edward, who led her to the bench and waited for her to be seated before sitting next to her.

'It's very pleasant here, don't you think?' she asked, surveying the view.

Edward looked around the park and saw couples and families eating picnics on the grass while others strolled along the paths, all of them strangers to him. He preferred quiet places like Rookhope, with its wide open spaces and fewer people, all of whom he knew, or the woodland surrounding Tommy's cottage. The park was not his idea of pleasant—he was only there to indulge Charlotte.

'You're very quiet, Edward. Is everything alright?'

'I'm a little warm, too. Would you mind if I remove my coat?'

'Of course, I wouldn't mind, silly. I would rather you were comfortable than pass out from the heat.'

Edward slipped off his coat, hung it over the back of the seat, and said, 'Thank you, that's better.'

'I hope you don't think I'm forward, Edward,' she said, 'but I feel as though there's a connection between us, and I would like to get to know you better. I know you're a busy man, but perhaps we could find a way to spend a little more time together?'

Edward had no idea what to say. Charlotte was a young, attractive, wealthy woman; any man would be lucky to be in her company. But it would be pointless for him to spend more time with her. Their blossoming friendship was based on deceit. His deceit. Because of his dual life, he had deliberately withheld information from her and let her believe he was a wealthy gentleman worthy of her attention. He had never taken their encounters seriously because every time they had met, he had been playing the role of a gentleman. She would never have looked at him twice if she'd met him as Edward Earle rather than Edward—the earl.

'I'm sorry if I have given you the impression that I might be interested in taking our friendship further, Charlotte,' he said, 'but I'm not a free man to go courting.'

'You're not married, are you? Oh, my goodness! I feel such a fool.' Charlotte swallowed, her chin trembling. 'Why didn't you tell me?'

'I'm not married—yet, but I soon shall be. I'm promised to another woman.'

Charlotte stared wide-eyed at him for a second and then lowered her head. When she lifted it, there were tears in her eyes.

'I'm very sorry, Charlotte. I didn't mean to upset you. Shall I walk you back to the orphanage?'

'Really, there's no need for that,' she said hastily. 'I know fine well where it is.'

She stood up and marched away without looking back.

Edward leaned forward and put his head in his hands, pondering what he had said or done to lead her on. He had always been polite and attentive in her company, but any gentleman would have acted in the same manner.

Although there was no future for them as a couple, Edward still felt terrible about lying to her to prevent her from getting close to him. He wasn't engaged to be married. He loved Dorothy Robson with all his heart, but there was no agreement between them, no engagement, nor would there be.

Chapter 36

Gateshead Fell
September 1770

The wind howled over the darkened moors. Low clouds obscured the moon and stars, making it difficult for the horses to pick a safe path over the boggy ground. Edward wondered if they had made a mistake coming out tonight. He had decided to try the toll road that crossed Gateshead Fell, part of the Great North Road, for the first time. It took longer to reach the highway than he'd expected, and it was late by the time they got there. Too late for most travellers to be out on the open roads. Most would be tucked up in a coaching inn, eating, drinking or sleeping soundly in their beds.

Edward and Tommy stopped in a dip about a hundred yards from the rough road that connected Durham to the town of Gateshead. This track was the main thoroughfare for journeying north and south through the region, used by merchants, the gentry, the Scots, and the locals by day; the locals knew better than to venture out into the wilderness at night.

No more than ten minutes had passed before Tommy nudged Edward and pointed to a pair of coach lamps in the distance. They readied to ride onto the road just seconds before the coach reached their hiding place.

Their horses leapt up the bank and stopped in the middle of the road, Edward's horse rearing at being pulled up sharply.

On seeing the highwaymen, the coachman whipped his horses so they would keep going, but the horses, trying to avoid a collision, veered to the edge of the road to pass. The cartwheel was precariously close to the edge of the road, and then the edge gave way under the weight of the coach, and the wheel went with it. Travelling at such high speed, the cart overturned, the horses screamed as they were pulled to a sudden halt and toppled over by the weight of the coach, and the coachman was flung high into the air.

Edward was horrified by what he saw. He went to the horses and loosened them from their harnesses so they could get to their feet. They appeared shaken but unhurt. Then, he looked through the coach window and saw a single occupant, a well-dressed gentleman with a gash to his head and blood flowing down the side of his face.

Tommy returned to the coach after finding the coachman several yards away. He shook his head. 'He's dead,' he said, 'but I found these.' He held up two shillings from the dead man's pocket.

Climbing onto the carriage, Edward opened the door and looked inside. 'The passenger is still breathing,' he said. 'Help me lift him out.'

'Out of the way, I'll do it,' said Tommy, climbing into the carriage. He lifted the man using one arm, and Edward pulled him out through the door and laid him down on the carriage. Tommy climbed out, lifted the man down, and set him on the grass at the side of the road.

Edward rifled through the man's pockets, which were empty, and removed a gold ring from his finger.

The man opened his eyes and looked directly into Edward's face.

'I know you,' he croaked.

Edward didn't recognise the man. He had no recollection of seeing him before, so he thought no more of his words, putting them down to confusion because the man had bumped his head.

Tommy nudged Edward and inclined his head, indicating they should leave, but before they did, Edward checked the coach for valuables and found a bag of coins that must have fallen from the man's pocket when the coach overturned.

'Come on, we should go,' said Tommy anxiously. 'What if another coach comes?'

They returned to their horses and rode onto the open moor towards home.

'Should we tell somebody about the accident?' asked Tommy. 'That man needs help.'

'No, we can't. As much as I would like to, we can't risk it. Nobody must know that we were over here tonight.'

'Aye, you're right. I suppose someone will come across him soon enough.'

A couple of days later, Edward was at his desk in the solicitor's office, carefully writing a will for a client while Mr Travis perused the newspaper.

His employer lifted his head and said, 'What a strange occurrence! A coach belonging to Mr Henry Harrison of Newcastle overturned on the road north of Chester-le-Street. He said a man helped him after the accident but then mysteriously disappeared. He swore it was Lord Malham from Durham, but Lord Malham was in London on business at the time.'

'How odd!' said Edward. 'Perhaps the man had suffered a concussion in the accident.'

'He did have injuries to his head as it happens. He may have been confused. You know, I've always thought you have a look of Lord Malham. I don't suppose you were anywhere near Chester-le-Street on Tuesday evening and helped a gentleman in distress?'

Edward laughed. 'The chance would be a fine thing. I haven't been further than Sunderland in months. You know, I would love to travel and see more of the world.'

'Ah! There are so many wonderful places to visit.'

Distracted from his newspaper, Mr Travis recounted tales of his trips to Scotland, Wales, France and Italy while Edward mulled over what the solicitor had said earlier. He knew that he looked very much like Lord Malham, and Lord Malham was well-known throughout the region.

Will that family likeness bring about my downfall?

He would have to be more careful to hide his face in the future whenever he went out at night.

Chapter 37

The Orphanage, Sunderland
September 1770

Sarah smiled brightly as she showed Edward into the orphanage and accompanied him to Mr Dunsmore's office. She knocked at the door and opened it for Edward to enter the room, where Mr Dunsmore was sitting at his desk, writing in a ledger.

'My Lord, I dinnae ken you were callin' today.' Mr Dunsmore rushed to his feet and shook hands with Edward. 'Please, tek a seat.'

Edward sat down, and Mr Dunsmore returned to his chair at the other side of the desk. He bent down, opened a drawer under the desk, and pulled out two crystal glasses and a bottle of Scotch.

'I believe congratulations are in order if I hear rightly,' he said, raising his eyebrows.

Edward had no idea what the man meant and kept his face impassive.

Mr Dunsmore poured a good measure of whisky into each

glass and said, 'Charlotte told me. I hope she didn't speak out of turn.'

Then, it dawned on Edward that Charlotte had told her brother-in-law about his fantasy engagement.

'Thank you,' said Edward.

'So, who is your intended? Would I know her?'

'Probably not. She lives a long way from Sunderland.'

'Ah, I don't suppose you see her verra much.'

'Not as often as I'd like,' said Edward ruefully.

'It must be a love match then. I'm pleased for you,' said Mr Dunsmore, holding up his glass. 'To your future together.'

'To our future,' said Edward, clicking glasses and pasting a smile on his face. He wished this engagement wasn't a fabrication of his own making and that he was about to marry Dorothy Robson. Nothing would make him happier.

He took a sip of the potent liquid.

'Now, back to business,' said Edward, pulling a pile of pound notes from his pocket.

After the donation had been recorded and Edward had been thanked profusely, Edward asked, 'How is Charlotte? I haven't seen her for a while.'

'Oh! Didn't ye ken? She's visitin' friends of the family in Scotland. It's lovely up there at this time of year. They're stayin' at their castle on the banks of Loch Tay just now. Shootin' and fishin'. They'll travel back to their townhouse in Edinburgh next month. Charlotte adores the shops in Edinburgh.'

'I've never been to Scotland, but I imagine it's a beautiful country with its rugged hills, glens and lochs. Please pass on my regards when you or your wife next write to her.'

'Aye, of course we will.'

Edward downed the whisky and rose to leave.

'She holds you in the highest regard, you know,' said Mr Dunsmore, the alcohol loosening his tongue. 'I did wonder if the two of you—'

'My heart was already promised to another when I met your sister-in-law. Charlotte is a wonderful woman. I'm sure she'll have no trouble finding a more suitable husband than me.'

Mr Dunsmore walked around to where Edward stood, and they shook hands again. 'I wish you well, Edward.'

Edward nodded before leaving the room. Lie after lie, he thought. *When will it end?*

Chapter 38

Durham Gaol
October 1770

After six days in prison, Edward was still dwelling on the betrayal, wondering who had informed the police. He sat on the bed and looked at the problem from a different perspective. *Who knows where I live?*

There was Sarah, who had helped Tommy when he'd been injured; Dorothy, who he had told; Mr Travis, the solicitor, who had held the deeds of Hawthorn Cottage until Tommy came of age to inherit it; Reverend Plunkett, the vicar from St Michaels, who had visited them in an attempt to get them to attend his church; and the estate's forester, known to him only as Jim, who had employed Tommy on occasion.

As far as he was aware, none of them knew about his illegal activities—except for Sarah.

But then he recalled the conversation with Mr Travis when he'd mentioned his likeness to Lord Malham after reading about the accident near Chester-le-Street. Mr Travis was a bright man. *Could he have worked out that I am, in fact, the highwayman?*

Also, Edward remembered the look on the vicar's face

when he'd seen him dressed as a gentleman at the orphanage. Edward knew that Mr Dunsmore could not be relied upon to keep a secret and doubted that the man would lie to a man of the cloth if questioned. *Could the Reverend have connected the gentleman he'd seen at the orphanage with the ungodly man in the woods and figured out how I am raising money to help the orphans?*

Every time he considered the options, he regretfully returned to Sarah Potts as the most likely suspect. He couldn't discount the fact that she knew they were highwaymen, and she knew where they lived. Logic told him that she was the one who had betrayed them.

Two guards came to their cell door.

'There's someone here to see you,' said the taller guard. 'You're to come with us.'

He unlocked the door, and the other guard came in, put handcuffs and shackles on the prisoners, and said, 'Follow me.'

Edward wondered who had come to see them, and then his heart sank when he realised that it was probably another witness who had come to identify them.

They left the prison building and stepped out into the yard, as they had done previously, but there was no sunshine this time. The sky was full of ominous dark clouds, and Edward had a dreadful feeling about what was about to happen.

He and Tommy waited with the guards, and soon, they were joined by the same policeman and prison warden, but a different gentleman stood beside them. Looking them up and down, the gentleman pointed his stick at Edward and said, 'I recognise this man. He is the one who stole my wife's jewellery when we were travelling on the Durham to Darlington road last month.'

'Are you certain, sir?' asked the policeman.

'Yes. There is no doubt in my mind whatsoever that this is the man.'

'And what about this man here?' The policeman pointed at Tommy.

'I can't say for certain as his accomplice stayed further away from our carriage, but he is a similar build so I would say that it is probably him.'

'Sir, please can you confirm that you are identifying these two men here as the two highwaymen who robbed you near the coaching inn at Rushyford?'

'Yes, I am. I want justice to be done. I doubt that I'll ever recover my wife's valuable jewellery, but I want these scoundrels punished for what they have done.'

Tommy looked at Edward in dismay.

Edward knew exactly how he felt. He didn't recognise the man accusing them of robbery either, and they had never been out on the Durham to Darlington road.

'Sir, you are mistaken,' said Edward. 'I have never laid eyes on you before and I have never been to Rushyford.'

'Calm down, Earle,' said the policeman. 'You'll get the chance to defend yourself in front of the judge tomorrow mornin'. Guards, take them back to their cell.'

When they were alone, Tommy said, 'I've never seen that man before in me life, never mind stolen owt off him. I didn't mind bein' accused of somethin' I'd done, Edward, but goin' to court and bein' hanged for somethin' I haven't done is—is—'

'I know,' said Edward, hugging his friend. 'It's not right.'

'What are we goin' to do?'

'There's little we can do. We should discuss what will happen tomorrow at the court and make sure that our stories are the same. Of course, we'll deny we were there because we weren't, but with a witness who sounds certain that he saw us, I don't think we'll have much success.'

'So, that's it, then. We're goin' to die.'

Edward hugged Tommy again. There was no doubt in his mind that that was precisely what was going to happen.

Tommy began to recite the Lord's Prayer over and over to himself. When he eventually stopped, the men spent the rest of the day quietly contemplating their circumstances and coming to terms with their fate.

Edward had no control over what would happen the following day and felt totally helpless. Desperately wanting to lighten the mood, he fished the pack of cards out from under the bed, and he and Tommy played late into the evening, their meals untouched by the door.

In the early hours of the morning, Edward heard someone whisper his name. A cloaked figure stood at the cell door, his face in shadow. Edward wondered if the guard who had taunted them had returned to seek revenge, and he poked Tommy with his elbow to wake him. He wanted Tommy to be by his side if they were about to be set upon.

'What is it?' asked Edward with trepidation.

A door opened in the distance, and Edward heard footsteps, two guards doing their rounds. The figure disappeared into the darkness.

When the guards had passed and the door slammed shut, the shadowy figure returned to the cell door and stepped back so his candle lighted his face.

'Jimmy Robson?' whispered Edward. 'Is that you?'

Edward stood up quickly and went to the door to look

closer.

'Aye, it's me,' said Jimmy.

'I can't tell you how good it is to see a friendly face. What are you doing here?'

'I've been workin' at the gaol for over a year now. I'm surprised our John didn't mention it. I went home for a few days, and when I came back to Durham, I saw the notice in the paper about you and your friend here,' he said, pointing to Tommy. 'Well, with you bein' a mate of our John's and our Dot bein' sweet on you, there's no way I can't let you stand trial tomorrow. They'd have me guts for garters if I let anythin' happen to you.'

Jimmy removed a bunch of keys from his belt and held up one of them.

Edward grinned. He couldn't believe their luck. Jimmy had come to help them escape.

'Does Dorothy know I'm here? What I'm accused of?' asked Edward.

'No, and she won't hear it from me. Innocent until proven guilty as far as I'm concerned.'

Edward would have hugged the man if they had not been separated by iron bars.

Jimmy turned the key in the lock, opened the cell door and waved his hand for them to follow him.

Quietly, they crept through the gaol. Most prisoners they passed were sleeping soundly in their cells, but a few turned their eyes towards them. One man looked like he would sound the alarm, but Tommy glared at him, and the prisoner thought better of it and lay back down on his mattress.

Jimmy unlocked the outer door. Two guards were standing in the yard, chatting to each other, and then they turned and walked towards the door. Jimmy closed it and quickly turned the key.

'Quick, come in here,' said Jimmy, who opened another door a little further down the passageway. They followed him into what Edward presumed to be the guards' room. A small fire burned in the grate, and beer bottles littered the table. Thankfully, no guards were resting in it.

They stood together behind the door in silence, hoping the men from the yard would not enter the room. They heard the outer door open and then close. Footsteps approached the guardroom door and then receded into the distance.

Jimmy breathed a sigh of relief. 'Come on, let's get you out of here,' he said. Cautiously, he opened the door and looked out. The passage was clear. Edward and Tommy followed him to the outer door, which Jimmy opened slightly and peered out into the dark yard, which was empty.

They ran over to the large wooden gates together. Jimmy removed the bar from the gates, and they gaped open. With a hand on Edward's shoulder, Jimmy wished them the very best of luck.

Edward nodded to Jimmy in thanks before he and Tommy slipped through the gateway into the streets of Durham. They were free at last.

Chapter 39

Durham
October 1770

Tommy saw a cartman he knew from Sunderland offloading fish on the narrow street leading down from the gaol.

'Are you headin' back to Sunderland, Bob?' asked Tommy, who sounded surprisingly calm considering he was a fugitive on the run.

'Tommy, isn't it? You needin' a ride, lad?'

'Aye, just to the Silksworth turn off, if you don't mind.' Nudging Edward, he said, 'Me and me friend here met some women at a tavern in the town last night. We were supposed to be stayin' with them for the night, but their husbands came back early and we had to make a run for it. I wouldn't be surprised if they come after us.'

The cartman laughed lewdly. 'There's some hessian sheets in the cart,' he said. 'You can hide under them if you want.' He laughed again as he lifted the last basket from the cart.

'Thanks, we owe you.'

When the cart was empty, they climbed in, lay down and pulled the sheets over themselves, peering out to see if anyone from the gaol was following.

As the cart bounced over the rough road, the smell of fish made Edward feel queasy. His heart was still racing from the escape, making it difficult to think clearly. He liked to work to a plan, to think about pitfalls and how to avoid them, and he reckoned that was why he had been a successful thief and highwayman until he had been betrayed.

But tonight, there was no plan, and Edward felt utterly at a loss. As soon as they left the town, he removed the hessian cover, sat upright, and breathed slowly and deeply to clear his head.

Tommy sat up, too and sighed loudly.

'Do you think it's wise to go home?' asked Edward. 'That's where they'll look for us first.'

'Aye, I dare say they will,' said Tommy. 'But we need to get our horses. We won't get far without them, will we?'

Tommy was right, and he needed to recover the money hidden in the cottage, too.

Edward knew they must avoid being seen as much as possible, as constables would search for them as soon as they learned of their escape. He needed to consider their options and determine their best chance of staying free.

They could flee the country. They could sail to France and live there, as many fugitives from England had done in the past. Tommy knew some of the sailors at the docks and could arrange transport, and he had money to pay. Mr Peters had taught him French, and he could speak the language fluently. France was looking good.

It's not like he or Tommy had any family to leave behind, but he did have friends he'd sorely miss, especially John, who had put himself at risk to help him, and Dorothy, whom he adored. *If I go to France, could I get word to them?*

They could ride to Scotland, but the Scots hated Englishmen; the Battle of Culloden, where the English massacred the Scottish clans, had not been forgotten. The Scots could lynch them just for being English, or if they discovered they were criminals, they might return them to Durham in chains and claim a reward for their capture.

They could go up into the Pennine hills and drift between Alston Moor and the steep-sided valleys of Weardale, Allendale and Teesdale, avoiding the settlements. Fewer people lived up there, and there weren't many lawmen either, so they were less likely to be captured in that area. He had ridden to Nenthead and Rookhope recently, so his presence there would not raise suspicions. He was sure John would help them at Nenthead, and he knew he could rely on the Robsons for food and shelter at Rookhope.

Edward reckoned their best chance of staying out of gaol would be to keep moving, but he didn't know how long they could keep that up. Hopefully, long enough for him to devise a better, longer-term plan.

His heart sank when he realised that he would no longer be able to help the children at the orphanage. He had been so proud of his achievements there. Mr Dunsmore would wonder why he had stopped making his payments, and Edward hoped he wouldn't think it was because of the misunderstanding with Charlotte in the park that day. He would never let anything so trivial stop him from helping the orphans.

The cart stopped, and Bob shouted, 'We're at the crossroads.'

Tommy and Edward jumped off the cart and thanked him for his help. The cartman drove away, chuckling, thinking he'd helped some philanderers escape from a romantic dalliance.

The day was breaking by the time they arrived at Hawthorn Cottage. Edward went inside and removed the money from under the loose floorboard while Tommy stuffed what little food he could find in his pockets. Edward took the blankets from their beds and handed one to Tommy.

'We'll need these if we're sleeping outdoors,' he said. 'We can roll them up and tie them behind the saddles.'

'So, do you know where we're going yet?' asked Tommy.

'Yes, I have a plan. We're going up into the hills.'

'That's want I wanted to hear.' Tommy slapped him on the back. 'It's good to know that brain of yours is workin' again.'

'Let's get the horses and be on our way,' said Edward.

As they saddled the horses, Tommy said, 'Shouldn't we hide somewhere until it gets dark?'

'Why?'

'Well, to get to the hills, we have to go through Durham, don't we?'

'We can cross the river at Chester-le-Street instead,' said Edward. 'The bridge there isn't as busy as the ones in Durham. The sooner we get away from here, the better.'

'I don't know how you remember all of them places and all of them roads,' said Tommy, getting onto his horse. 'I could get lost goin' to the netty.'

Edward chuckled, knowing that Tommy wasn't exaggerating very much. He mounted his mare, and they set off on their journey westwards with the weak autumn sun on their backs.

Chapter 40

Weardale
October 1770

Edward and Tommy took the longer, northern route to avoid the town of Durham as they travelled towards the Pennine hills. They knew that news of their escape would spread quickly. A few people stared at or eyed them suspiciously before turning their backs, pretending they hadn't seen them.

Edward knew that highwaymen who stole from the rich, like himself, were not regarded as a threat by the poor. They were more likely to consider him a hero for taking wealth away from the wealthiest people in society. Indeed, they certainly would if they knew that the proceeds from his deeds were helping those in need.

He grimaced as he remembered Sarah likening him to Robin Hood, the legendary hero. He still couldn't understand why she would have told the police he was a highwayman and led them to his door when she had been concerned that his capture would adversely affect the children.

So, why on earth had she done it?

Even though he considered the threat of the villagers revealing their whereabouts small, he decided they should

206

lay low for the rest of the day and continue their journey at nightfall, so they rested by a stream and took turns to nap.

They rode through the night and covered a lot of ground, and dawn broke as they reached Stanhope. Edward saw a discarded newspaper on a bench in the marketplace and leaned down to grab it, and then he and Tommy continued riding until they reached the woods at Rookhope, away from prying eyes. They dismounted and let the horses rest by the burn.

Edward unrolled his blanket and sat down, eager to read the paper to find out if news of their escape had been published. He stopped turning the pages when he reached the fourth page.

'What does it say?' asked Tommy, looking over Edward's shoulder at the paper even though he couldn't read it.

Edward read aloud two consecutive articles.

"County Durham, Escaped from Justice! Edward Earle, who was born in Rookhope, in Weardale, in the said County, is about 23 years of age, about six feet high, of a fair complexion, long dark brown hair, which he sometimes wears tied behind with a black ribbon, and has green eyes. The said Earle, is a slim build and walks tall and upright; on the 19th and 20th days of this month, he wore a dark-coloured lapelled fustian coat with horn buttons with silver knops in the middle, light-coloured drawers, and silver buckles at his shoes. He has lately been seen at Chester-le-Street and Lanchester, in the said County of Durham, and generally rides on a brown mare. Whoever will apprehend the said Edward Earle so that he may be secured in any of His Majesty's gaols, shall, upon notice given to Jonathan Hope, Deputy Clerk of the Peace for the said County, receive a reward of Ten Guineas, to be paid by Mr Thompson, Attorney at Law, in Durham.

Also, Thomas Bell, accomplice to the said Earle, who was born in Sunderland, in the said County, is about 24 years of age, about five feet ten inches high, of a ruddy complexion, straight and short mid-brown hair. The said Bell is stoutly made; he has a round face, a dimple on his chin, and brown eyes. He is missing his left hand from an accident and sometimes wears a wooden hand in its place. He wore a brown pea jacket, brown waistcoat and striped drawers, with a pair of small oval carved buckles at his shoes. He is likely to be in the company of the aforementioned Edward Earle, and generally rides a grey mare. Whoever will apprehend the said Thomas Bell so that he may be secured in any of His Majesty's gaols, shall, upon notice given to Jonathan Hope, Deputy Clerk of the Peace for the said County, receive a reward of Five Guineas, to be paid by Mr Thompson, Attorney at Law, in Durham."

'God's blood!' said Tommy. 'Who'd have thought I'd be worth five guineas? I've never had more than a few shillings to me name.'

Edward didn't share Tommy's delight at hearing the price on their heads. Fifteen guineas was a fortune to most people. Even their friends might be tempted to hand them over to the authorities for that sum of money.

They would have to be even more cautious than he'd thought and try to remain hidden as much as possible during the daytime. Luckily, their horses were used to being ridden at night.

His imminent concern for their safety meant that Edward failed to notice the report of the death of his half-brother, the heir to the Granby estate, on the following page of the newspaper.

Tragic Accident, Granby Estate Heir Trampled to Death, on Saturday last past. James Worthington Malham, the twenty-

nine-year-old son and heir of Lord Malham of Granby Hall near Durham was leading the Granby Hunt when a tragic accident occurred. His horse fell whilst jumping a hedgerow and landed badly, trapping the young Malham beneath it when it fell. The riders who followed Malham over the hurdle did not see him lying in their path until it was too late, and their hunters had trodden on him. Other horses fell whilst trying to avoid him and unseated their riders, who suffered minor injuries. It is fortunate that there were no more fatalities. Both the young Malham and his horse were trampled to death. Lord Malham was present at the hunt when the accident happened. He is said to be distraught over the death of his son. The funeral service took place on Wednesday last at Durham Cathedral, with the Right Reverend Benjamin Ashton, Bishop of Durham, presiding. The event was very well attended, with the great and the good of Durham County and the neighbouring counties of Northumberland and Yorkshire turning out to show their respects. Malham's body was later interred in the family vault at Granby Hall.

Chapter 41

'What are we goin' to have for our teas?' asked Tommy, his stomach rumbling.

'There are a few hazel trees upstream. The nuts should be ripe at this time of year.'

'Good! I'll go and fetch some.'

While Tommy went to collect hazelnuts, Edward sat by the river contemplating how they could survive with as little help from friends as possible; he didn't want to endanger the Robsons. He knew they didn't read the newspapers, but they may have heard about his arrest and escape from somebody else. News spread quickly, and because he was a Rookhope man, he feared it might have reached the village already.

He decided that they should stay hidden in the woods for a couple of nights and fend for themselves before going to the farmhouse for supplies, and then they could hide out again for a few nights before going to John's at Nenthead. He guessed the news would take longer to reach Nenthead, but not much longer because the lead miners walked between the dales for work every week. As John knew about his illegal activities,

210

Edward was confident he could rely on his help regardless of whether or not he had heard about his arrest and escape.

Tommy came back carrying his hat.

'There's loads of nuts lying on the ground under them trees. I didn't know how many to pick up, so I filled me hat and me pockets.'

'Good! We'll have plenty to eat tonight.'

Edward took one, picked up a rock and crushed the shell. He removed the nut and ate it, and then Tommy copied him awkwardly using one hand.

'They're nice, these,' said Tommy.

Edward nodded and took a handful.

Tommy continued to eat the rest.

When darkness fell, they took their blankets and lay down to sleep behind a fallen tree trunk, out of sight of the path by the river. Edward was a little concerned that they couldn't hide their horses that grazed nearby, but that didn't stop him from falling into a deep sleep.

The next day, Tommy sat up and groaned.

'What's wrong?' asked Edward.

'Them nuts are playin' havoc with me guts. I'm not eatin' them again.'

'You did have a lot of them. Maybe we could catch a fish for tea tonight.'

'Don't talk about food!' begged Tommy, clutching his belly and running behind a tree.

Edward shook the blankets and rolled them up, wondering how they would pass their time out here. Fishing seemed to be the perfect activity because it would give them something to do and provide them with food.

He couldn't think of a way to construct a fishing net in

the woods, and they didn't have any hooks, so he decided they needed spears, which he could make. He searched for two fallen branches that were narrow but a good length and took them back to the riverside, where Tommy sat looking miserable.

Taking his knife from his pocket, Edward unsheathed it, scraped the end of the wood to make a sharp point, and then did the same with the second piece of wood.

'Come on,' said Edward, 'Let's see who can catch a fish first.'

Tommy's eyes lit up at the challenge, and he grabbed a spear from Edward's hand, removed his boots and socks, and waded into the burn.

Edward followed him, being careful not to slip on the algae-covered stones that formed the riverbed. They stood quietly, the cold water flowing around their lower legs, for what seemed like hours before Tommy jabbed his spear into the water.

'Missed it!' he said. 'It was a big one, an' all.'

When Edward could no longer feel his feet, he said, 'Let's take a break and try again later. Fancy a game of cards?'

In the afternoon, they went back into the river and within half an hour, Edward skewered a rainbow trout large enough to feed them both. They lit a small fire and cooked the fish over the flames, and Edward thought it was the best fish he'd ever tasted.

The following day, Edward suggested they go to the Robsons' house. They washed in the river and brushed down their clothes so they didn't look like they'd been sleeping rough, saddled their horses and rode to the farm.

'Ed, is that you?' asked Mrs Robson when he knocked at the farmhouse door and entered the kitchen.

'Aye, it's him, Bessie. He keeps turnin' up like a bad penny,' said Mr Robson, laughing at his own joke.

Edward looked at the ageing couple sitting at the table. Seeing just the two of them there was strange when this house had always been so full of children. He knew from John that most of his siblings had left home or worked away during the week.

But where was Dorothy?

'That's a fine welcome when he's hardly through the door,' said Mrs Robson. 'Sit down, lad.'

'I have a friend with me. Is it alright if he comes in?'

The couple looked at each other.

'Aye, show him in,' said Mr Robson.

Edward went to the door, and Tommy followed him into the house.

'Good afternoon, Mr and Mrs Robson, Edward's told me a lot about you,' said Tommy with a smile.

'Has he now?' asked Mrs Robson. 'Come in and sit down, I'll make a fresh pot of tea. I hope you're hungry 'cos I baked yesterday.'

She put the kettle over the fire to boil, then went to the pantry and brought out a tatie cake, a couple of buttered scones, and some ginger biscuits.

Edward and Tommy were ravenous and tucked into the food before the tea was stewed.

'Didn't you stop for food on the way over?' asked Mr Robson.

'No, not today,' said Edward. 'I didn't want to spoil my appetite.'

'This is delicious, Mrs Robson,' said Tommy, his mouth full of tatie cake. 'I don't think I've ever eaten anythin' this good before.'

Mrs Robson smiled at Tommy and said, 'You can come here again, lad.'

'Why is it that you've come, Ed?' asked Mr Robson. 'Our Dot's not here.'

Edward's heart sank. 'If you don't mind me asking, where is she?' he asked.

'She's stayin' at our Deborah's over at Blanchland. Deborah had a little lad last week. Dot's helpin' her out 'til she's back on her feet.'

Edward wondered if they could go to Blanchland and see Dorothy. It wasn't far from Rookhope. But as much as he wanted to see her, he couldn't put her and another family at risk, especially one with a newborn baby in the house.

'It's a shame we'll not see her. If we return in a few weeks, will she be back?' asked Edward hopefully.

'So, it was the lass that you came callin' for. All bein' well, she should be back by then.' Looking at his wife, Mr Robson said, 'I told you he'd be back for her, Bessie, didn't I?'

'Aye, an' it's just as well he is,' said Mrs Robson. 'She wasn't herself after you went the last time, Ed. Moping about for weeks, she was. And then she's not set eyes on you for over a year. Well, we didn't know what to think.'

It was clear to Edward that the Robsons thought he'd come to propose to their daughter and wished that was the reason for his visit, not that he was an escaped convict on the run seeking food and refuge.

'Aye, come back in a few weeks, lad,' said Mr Robson, winking at him.

The plates on the table were empty.

'By, you weren't kiddin' when you said you had an appetite!'

said Mrs Robson, who looked rather pleased that the young men had enjoyed the meal.

'Would you mind if we stayed in the barn tonight and we'll head home in the morning?'

'Of course, you can. You'll have your breakfast with us in the morning an' all and I'll pack you some food for your journey.'

'Thank you, Mrs Robson,' said Edward. 'That's very kind of you.'

The men went outside into the barn and lay their blankets on the hay. It was the most comfortable place they had slept for a while, and they had a good night's rest.

Chapter 42

Weardale
October 1770

Edward and Tommy left the safety of the farm and rode over the hill from Rookhope to Cowshill, avoiding most of the Weardale villages and reducing their chances of being seen. However, as they trotted past the inn at Cowshill, Edward felt the stares of the local lead miners and avoided eye contact. He was sure that the men had recognised them.

'I don't think we have any friends there,' said Tommy as they left the village.

'I agree,' said Edward, with a sinking feeling in the pit of his stomach.

They continued over Killhope, crossing the county boundary at the top of the hill, and rode down to John's cottage near Nenthead.

Outside the cottage, they dismounted and left their horses in the small paddock behind the house. Edward was pleased that they couldn't be seen from the road.

John approached them as they walked to his door, and he looked from one to the other.

'John, this is Tommy Bell from Silksworth.'

'Tommy, this is John Robson from Rookhope.'

The men shook hands.

'I wasn't expectin' to see you for a while yet,' said John. 'Is somethin' up?'

'Aye, that's one way of puttin' it,' said Tommy.

'Jenny's resting upstairs. Did you hear that she had a little lad?'

Edward shook his head. 'Congratulations!' he said. With everything that had happened lately, he had forgotten all about the baby. 'What's his name?'

'We called him John.'

Edward smiled, thinking that there would be another generation of John Robsons in the family, and if the boy turned out anything like his father and grandfather, he'd be a decent man.

'Come in, but keep your voices down,' said John. 'She didn't get any sleep last night with the little 'un.'

Edward and Tommy followed John into the house and sat around the table.

'So, what's wrong?' asked John.

'I'm sorry to bring trouble to your door,' said Edward, 'but Tommy and I were arrested and taken to Durham Gaol. We escaped a few days ago. We're wanted men.'

'Bloody hell!' said John under his breath. 'So, there'll be men out lookin' for you.'

'Probably the authorities and maybe a few individuals as well, wanting to claim the reward,' said Edward calmly. 'There's a price on our heads.'

John sat with his mouth open, unable to believe what he'd heard.

'What can I do to help?' he asked.

'Do you know of any empty buildings around here where we could hide out for a few days? Somewhere secluded?'

'Aye, there's a place between here and Coalcleugh. It's a small farmstead. Not been lived in for years. Nobody goes anywhere near the place. They say it's haunted. The last fella who lived there hanged himself in the kitchen.'

'It sounds ideal,' said Edward.

'I'm not stayin' in no haunted house,' said Tommy, raising his voice.

'Shush, Tommy. I'll be with you. It'll be alright.'

Tommy didn't look convinced.

John gave them directions to the house. 'There's a spring up there for water, but you'll need to take some food with you. I'll have a look and see what I can find.'

'Thanks, John. Will you tell Jenny about us?'

'Aye, I'll have to tell her. If there's food missin', she'll ask questions. But you know you can trust her, Ed. She thinks the world of you. It was your little enterprise that gave us the means to get married.'

John filled a bag with an assortment of bread and pies that Jenny had baked and carrots and apples from his garden.

'That should be enough for three or four days,' he said, handing the bag to Edward. 'Be careful up there. You'll have a good view of anyone comin' from the Durham side, which is the most likely, but you'll not get much notice if they come down from the Alston side.'

'Thank you, John. I owe you.'

The farmhouse stood on a high plateau on the moor, and a patch of green grass gave away the location of the spring. The house looked like it hadn't been lived in for fifty years or more. The stone-tiled roof was still in place but sagged on either side of a central beam. Ivy climbed the sandstone walls and covered the windows on the front of the building. A barn had been built on the side of the house, and they led their horses inside and untacked them. The hay was old and dusty, but the animals nibbled at it anyway.

Inside the house, Edward wandered around the darkened rooms. Most of the furniture was still in place—a range, a table and two chairs in the kitchen, two old armchairs, a cupboard and a table in the parlour, and two wooden beds with mattress ticks stuffed with feathers in the bedrooms upstairs.

Wondering why the house was still furnished, Edward thought it would be difficult to remove the larger items due to the remoteness of the site, or maybe people really did believe that the house was haunted and were too scared to enter the property.

Edward didn't fear ghosts. He had never seen one himself and was sceptical that they existed. He went back outside, where Tommy waited for him, reluctant to go inside the house.

'What's it like in there?' asked Tommy. 'Did you see the ghost?'

'No, it's just an old house. There's nothing to fear. Come in and see for yourself.'

Tommy followed Edward, his face pale and his lips trembling. He shrieked as a mouse ran over his foot and disappeared into a gap between the wooden floorboards.

'Do we have to stay here?' asked Tommy. 'Couldn't we go back to the woods and sleep there again? I'd rather be outside.'

'It's safer to hide indoors, Tommy. Nobody will ever know we're here as long as we don't light the fire.'

'And nobody will find us if we die up here.'

'Who said anything about dying?' said Edward.

'You heard what John said. They'll be comin' to get us soon and take us back to Durham to stand trial, and that's if we don't die of fright before then. We goin' to die one way or t'other.'

Edward reached into the bag John had given him and took out a meat and potato pie. He had discovered years ago that the best way to divert Tommy's attention was through food.

'Sit down,' said Edward. 'You'll feel better after you've had something to eat.'

That night, he shared a room with Tommy, knowing how Tommy feared sleeping alone in the dark, but Edward didn't sleep. He was worried that someone would discover their hideout, and he spent the night listening to sounds outside.

They stayed in the farmhouse for four nights before their food ran out, and then they returned to John's cottage for more supplies.

When they reached the house, they saw John walking up the hill from Nenthead after his shift at the smelt mill, and they rode down to meet him.

'There was a constable at the door yesterday asking about you two,' said John. 'Somebody from Cowshill told him he'd seen you ridin' in this direction. Me and Jenny said we'd never seen you passin' if you'd come down this road.'

'Thanks, John. We'll get away from here. I don't want to put you and your family at risk. But would you mind if I bothered you for some more food before we go?'

'No problem, Ed.'

John went inside and refilled the bag for Edward, and when he returned, he said, 'Keep yourselves safe'.

As they rode away from John, Edward felt uneasy. If a constable had been knocking at doors along the routes that they may have taken, they couldn't risk going back the same way. He decided leaving the roads and taking to the open fells would be safer. At Killhope, they turned their horses onto an old track that led to Allenheads, riding slowly, taking care to keep to the path to avoid the countless black pools on the peaty moorland.

Dark clouds accumulated above their heads, and as they descended into the village of Allenheads, the clouds burst, and sheets of water washed over them, obscuring their view. The flooded path quickly turned into a river and was treacherous underfoot.

'We should take shelter until this passes,' shouted Edward. 'There's an inn over this way.'

Outside the inn, they jumped down from their mounts, tethered them outside, and ran indoors. The landlord was talking to a young boy, probably father and son, judging by their ages and similarity in looks, thought Edward.

The man eyed them suspiciously. 'I haven't seen you in here before,' he said.

'We were riding through the village when the rain started. We're seeking shelter until it passes.' Edward took some money from his pocket and said, 'We'll have a pint of ale each while we wait if you'd be so kind.'

Seeing the coins in Edward's hand, the landlord poured the drinks. 'Where are you headed?' he asked.

'Alston,' said Edward, lying with ease. His intention had been to find a hiding place near Allenheads for a few days before returning to Rookhope.

The man whispered something to the boy, and the boy left and went out the back to their private rooms, Edward presumed.

The men sat at a table and savoured their drinks, glad of a dry place to sit until the rain subsided. Through the window, they spied a constable running towards the inn with the boy by his side.

Edward and Tommy ran outside, untied their horses and leapt into the saddles.

The horses sensed the riders' urgency and galloped up the hill, passing the open-mouthed constable and boy, and they kept going at speed for several miles before they slowed to a walk and continued down into the Rookhope Valley.

In the distance, Edward heard horses' hooves travelling fast and men shouting. He looked over his shoulder and saw a group of riders following—about six of them.

Edward hadn't thought about where to go when he'd left Allenheads. To avoid the constable, he had instinctively headed towards Rookhope. He kicked Brandy and galloped up the fell towards Hunstanworth, with Tommy right behind him.

Their horses ran as fast as they could through the bracken and heather, jumping small streams and gulleys in their path. The distance between them and the other horses widened.

Edward panicked when he could no longer hear Ghost's hooves behind him, and he glanced back to see Tommy lying flat on the ground, Ghost standing over him. He turned around and was relieved to see Tommy was winded from the fall but unhurt.

He held out his hand and helped Tommy back onto Ghost, noticing that the men were gaining ground. They galloped their horses up the hill, and the men soon disappeared from sight. He was grateful for the stamina, speed and fitness of Brandy and Ghost, which far surpassed that of the horses chasing them.

They returned to the road to avoid leaving tracks across the fell for their pursuers to follow, and before they reached the village of Hunstanworth, they doubled back onto another track over the fell that led to Rookhope.

Happy that the men were no longer following them, they slowed to a walk and let the horses cool off on the descent into the village.

'By! That was close,' said Tommy.

'Too close,' replied Edward.

'Where are we goin' now? Even the haunted house was better than bein' chased like that. They could have at least had the decency to let us finish our drinks.'

Edward laughed. Thinking out loud, he said, 'We've been seen at Cowshill and at Allenheads. Those men saw us heading towards Hunstanworth and may have seen us turn towards Rookhope. Soon, there will be men searching all over this area for us. We need to get away from here and be seen somewhere else.'

'We could go back to Sunderland. They won't be lookin' for us there, and it's been ages since I've seen Sarah.'

'I know you think a lot about Sarah, Tommy, but we can't trust her.'

'I still say that you're wrong about her.'

'Let's not disagree. We have to work out what to do next to save our necks.'

Tommy lowered his eyes and followed Edward through the village and back to the woods where they had spent their first few nights on the run undetected.

'We'll stay here until nightfall,' said Edward. 'Then, under the cover of darkness, we'll ride over to Teesdale and then

223

on to Darlington. We'll make sure that we're seen there and then return up here. Try and get some sleep now, Tommy. It's going to be a long night.'

Chapter 43

White Hall Farm, Rookhope
November 1770

Edward and Tommy had travelled for almost two weeks, spending only a few days in one place. They were tired and weary. The nights were cold, and they struggled to sleep outdoors, even in their clothes and blankets. The thought of the Robsons' barn drew them back to Rookhope, and they rode into the yard in the murky dusk.

'Who's there?' shouted Mr Robson from the doorway.

'It's just us, Mr Robson. Edward Earle and my friend, Tommy.'

'Put the horses in the front field and get yourselves inside. It's freezin' out here tonight.' He went inside and closed the door.

They attended to the horses and entered the house, where a blazing fire burned in the grate, and the smell of beef stew greeted them.

After Mrs Robson placed a bowl of steaming stew and a mug of ale in front of each of them, she said, 'You've come back a bit soon. We're not expecting our Dot until tomorrow.'

'That's fine Mrs Robson. We'll wait. Would you mind if we

stay in the barn again?'

'You and that barn. It's far too cold to sleep out there tonight. There's an empty bedroom upstairs with our Dot being away. You can stay in there if you don't mind sharing.'

'That's very kind of you, thank you.'

Mr Robson had stayed quiet as the men ate, and when they finished, he said, 'Is there any truth in what I've been hearin'?'

Edward's stomach lurched. 'What have you heard?' he asked.

'Joseph Patterson walked all the way up here just to tell us that you and him were highwaymen and had escaped from Durham Gaol.'

Edward looked the man in the eyes and said, 'It's all been a huge misunderstanding.'

'I told you that would be the case, didn't I?' said Mrs Robson to her husband. 'Ed would never do anythin' to hurt anyone.'

The Robsons took him at his word, and the subject was not revisited that evening. Edward hated lying to the people dearest to him, but if he had confessed, they would have asked him to leave, and if that had happened, he wouldn't be able to see Dorothy.

With full stomachs, Edward and Tommy slept in a proper bed with pillows, sheets and blankets that night. Whether it was the ale, the warmth or the feeling of safety that made them sleep well, Edward didn't know, but he was grateful for a good night's rest.

The following day, Edward was in the yard and saw a horse and cart approach the farm. As it drew closer, he recognised Deborah sitting up front, and she was cradling her baby in her arms. He was sure he could see Dorothy in the back.

When the horse and cart pulled into the yard, the Robsons

came outside to greet their daughters and meet their new grandson while their son-in-law took care of his horse. Deborah was swiftly ushered into the house by her parents.

Edward caught up with Dorothy and placed his hand on her arm. 'Dorothy—'

She turned and looked up into his bright green eyes, and he inhaled sharply at the look in hers. Love or desire—he wasn't sure.

He had known for years that Dorothy admired him. As far as she knew, he was a clerk in a solicitor's office, a bachelor, and a family friend—a man she would consider a suitable husband.

He'd strung her along despite the choices he had made in his life. He could have married her years ago and had a family of his own by now, but instead, he had chosen a life of crime to help orphaned children.

He had to tell Dorothy he couldn't give her what she wanted—love, marriage, children.

'What is it, Edward?' she asked.

'May I accompany you for a walk?'

'I suppose so.'

'Is there something wrong?' he asked, surprised by her petulant tone.

'Is there somethin' wrong?' she scoffed. 'Aye, there's somethin' wrong. After our John's weddin' night, I thought we wanted the same thing. I thought we'd be the next couple to get married, but you up and left, and I haven't seen you for a year and a half! A year and a half, Edward, without a word. That's what's wrong.'

'I'm sorry, Dorothy. Really, I am.'

He smiled a charming smile and held out his arm, and he

227

was relieved when she took it and smiled back at him. His heart melted. He wanted so much to take her into his arms and kiss her, as he had done in the past, but he couldn't. He'd come to tell her they could not be wed, knowing he would break her heart, but he had to do it.

Until he told her the truth of the matter, she would never consider courting another man, and she must because he could never be her husband.

They walked for nearly a mile before Edward broke the silence.

'Let's sit by the river for a while.'

They sat on a fallen tree trunk beside the riverbank and watched the fast-flowing water hurtling downstream.

'Dorothy, we've been friends for such a long time and you know that there has always been an understanding between us.'

She nodded, her eyes large. 'I think I know what you're goin' to say, Edward, and the answer is yes!'

She got to her feet and kissed him on his lips.

Edward stood up immediately and said, 'No! Oh, Dorothy! What have I done?'

'What is it, Edward? Don't you want to marry me?'

'Please sit.' Sitting down again, facing her, he stroked her hair and said softly, 'I want to marry you so much, Dorothy, but I can't.'

'Why not?'

Edward swallowed. He didn't know what to say. He couldn't tell her the real reason, but he couldn't lie to her either.

'Are you married to somebody else?' she asked. 'Is that it?'

'No,' he said, shaking his head emphatically. 'I'm not married.'

'Then, what is it? What's stoppin' you from marryin' me?'

Edward looked down at his feet. He had never felt so uncomfortable in his life. Her hand lifted his chin so that he looked into her eyes.

'What is it?' she asked. 'I need to know.' Her blue eyes implored him to answer her question and relieve her misery.

'My lifestyle is not suited to taking a wife,' he said.

'What does that mean? Oh! Do you prefer men to women?'

'No! Struth!'

He put his head in his hands. He had no option but to tell her the truth. Excuses wouldn't work, not with Dorothy. They knew each other too well, and after the years she had waited for him, he owed her the truth.

He took her hands in his and looked into her eyes. 'You might find this shocking, Dorothy. Are you sure you want to know?'

'Yes. Just tell me, please.'

'I'm a felon. As well as working as a clerk, I burgle houses and rob people.'

Dorothy's mouth opened and then closed, and she started to laugh.

'I'm serious, Dorothy.'

She looked at him like she was seeing him for the first time.

'Don't you see?' he pleaded. 'I can't take a wife when I could be caught at any moment. And if I was convicted, I'd be strung up for what I've done.'

'Why do you do it?' she asked. 'You've got a good job. You don't need to steal.'

'I don't do it for myself. I give the proceeds to the orphanage in Sunderland. I do it for the children.'

Dorothy stood in front of Edward, who was still seated on

the tree trunk, and she wrapped her arms around his body and held him. His arms went around her, and he held her tightly, his head against her chest.

He had expected Dorothy to be horrified by what he'd done or to at least be angry with him, yet she was comforting him. *How could she react this way?*

Edward was experiencing so many thoughts and emotions. He was relieved that Dorothy knew about his secret life at last, surprised by her reaction, and frightened that he'd brought her into his confidence.

He didn't realise he was crying until Dorothy wiped the tears from his cheeks with her hand.

Her face just inches away from his, she said, 'Edward, what you are doin' is both gallant and foolish. Why don't you put an end to it now? Nobody need ever know what you've done. We could be wed and have children of our own for you to care for.'

What can I say to that?

Dorothy was offering him a way out. A life with a wife, a home and a family. But they wouldn't be able to stay in County Durham, not when there was a price on his head.

'Edward, say somethin', please,' she begged.

He looked into her eyes and saw pure love. *Why am I so afraid of it?* He wondered if he had spent too much of his life unloved that he couldn't accept it anymore.

'I love you, Edward, and I know you love me,' she said. 'Give me one good reason why we shouldn't get married.'

He shook his head slowly and watched the light fade in her eyes, and the smile disappeared from her face.

'There's more to it than I've told you.' He took her hands in his again and held them firmly, not wanting to let go. 'I was arrested for highway robbery and I escaped from gaol. I'm a wanted man and there's a price on my head.'

Dorothy gasped.

'The police know what I've done,' he continued, 'and they have a witness who'll say we stole from him, even though we didn't. If I get caught again, Dorothy, I'll be hanged.'

Dorothy shook her head slowly. 'No!' she said. 'That can't happen.'

She stood up, and Edward got to his feet, too.

'I love you, Edward,' she said. 'I've always loved you. What can we do to keep you safe?'

'Tommy and I were thinking about going to France.'

'France,' she repeated. 'I'll come with you—if you want me to?'

Edward could not believe it. Dorothy knew everything about him, yet she was prepared to leave her family home to be with him. He didn't deserve her.

But how can I refuse her when I want her so much?

He took her into his arms, and they kissed as though it might be the last time they ever saw each other.

Chapter 44

White Hall Farm, Rookhope
November 1770

When they returned to the farm, Dorothy went to the kitchen to help her mother with dinner, and Edward went over to Tommy in the farmyard, where he was turning the handle of a grindstone for Mr Robson, who was sharpening the blades on some scythes. When the last one was finished, Mr Robson thanked Tommy for his help and took the tools back to the barn.

'We'll leave first thing in the morning,' whispered Edward. 'We'll go to Sunderland and sail to France. Dorothy's coming with us.'

Tommy's mouth opened, but no words came out.

'I know she'll slow us down,' said Edward, 'but I want her to come. She knows everything about me and she still wants to be with me.'

Even as he said the words, he still didn't believe them.

'Fair enough,' said Tommy. 'What about her family? Do they know what you're plannin' to do?'

Edward looked sheepish. Mr and Mrs Robson would be upset when they discovered Dorothy had gone away with him without a ring on her finger, and he hoped that they would forgive him for what they'd done when they knew the reason.

'She said she'd leave them a note.'

Tommy tutted and shook his head.

'I know, they deserve better than that,' said Edward. 'But I can't tell them what's happening. They'd ask too many questions, and they might stop her from coming with me. The less they know the better until we're safe in France.'

After dinner, Edward and Tommy said goodnight to the family and went outside. Edward looked warily around the yard, sensing danger.

'Why don't you sleep in the hay loft above the byre?' he suggested. 'I'll sleep in the barn. That way, if there's anyone about, at least one of us will have a chance to get away.'

'Aye, alright,' said Tommy, and walked towards the byre.

Edward lay down in the barn and thought about the following day. He would take Dorothy away from Weardale, sail with her to France, and marry her at the first opportunity. Then, they would spend the rest of their lives together. He was excited at the prospect. Eventually, he closed his eyes and drifted off to sleep.

He stirred. A noise woke him, and he sat bolt upright, listening carefully, his heart thumping in his chest. He heard footsteps. Somebody was outside—at least one, perhaps more. The police had finally caught up with them, he thought.

Edward had slept in his clothes. He pulled on his shoes and went to the door, where he peered through the gap in the wooden slats. The moon was bright, and he could see the shadow of a man behind the cart and the head of a man hiding behind the farmyard wall. At the back of the barn, there was a small gap where the wood had rotted, and on his belly, he wriggled through it, leapt the dry-stone wall, and ran up the field towards a small sandstone quarry. He hid behind some juniper bushes growing in the quarry bottom and listened for the sound of movement nearby.

He wished he had his pistol with him. He had never intentionally wanted to hurt anyone, but if it meant he could escape, he would take a shot at a constable—returning to the gaol would mean certain death.

The night was quiet. Beads of sweat sat on Edward's brow, reflecting the moonlight. He wiped them away with his sleeve. The only sound he could hear was his heart pounding in his chest, not from exertion but from fear—a primal fear of being hunted and knowing that his life would soon be over.

Now that he was promised to Dorothy, he had so much more to lose. His capture would mean he was unlikely to see her again, and the hope of spending his life with her would be extinguished forever.

A net was dropped over him, and he yelled. He was trapped. He fought to free himself, clawing at the net, but couldn't tear it or lift it off him. Edward was physically exhausted when the two men climbed down from the top of the quarry, and he huddled on the ground. That was it. He had been captured.

Through his tears, he looked at the men but didn't recognise them.

'We've got you at last!' said the larger man triumphantly.

'You're a difficult man to track down, Edward Earle,' said the smaller one, sitting on the grass before him.

Edward was puzzled by their tweed outfits and their manner. They didn't look or act like policemen, and they were in no hurry to handcuff him and take him back to Durham Gaol.

'Who are you?' he asked.

'Ah, yes. Apologies. We should have introduced ourselves,' replied the smaller one, who appeared to be in charge. 'I'm James Brown and this is my colleague, George Baker. We work for Lord Malham.'

'Lord Malham? Surely, he doesn't need the reward money?' Edward laughed at the absurdity of the situation.

'You may be aware that Lord Malham's son was killed in an accident recently.'

Edward shook his head. 'No. I'm sorry to hear it. But what's that got to do with me?'

'Lord Malham knows that you are his son. It's obvious just by looking at you, and nobody could dispute it.'

Standing up again, the man said, 'If we remove the net, will you promise you won't run?'

Edward nodded and wiped his face.

The two men carefully removed the net from Edward, and the larger one tied it in a bundle.

'Lord Malham has asked that we take you to him to discuss a proposal.'

'Does he know that I'm wanted by the police?'

'Yes, his Lordship is aware of your present circumstances.'

'He doesn't intend to hand me over to the authorities, does he?'

'No! Nothing could be further from his mind. He's already lost one son. He does not want to lose another.'

'I should leave a note for my friends to let them know where I've gone.'

'We'll pass the farm on the way down to the coach. It's waiting for us at Stotsfieldburn. We'll wait for you in the yard until you're done.'

At White Hall Farm, Edward wrote a note to the Robsons to

inform them that Lord Malham had summoned him to go to Granby Hall and that they should not be concerned for him, and he left it on the kitchen table.

He would have liked to tell Dorothy in person, but she would be asleep upstairs in her room next to her parents' room. He couldn't risk being seen creeping into or out of her bedroom at night.

He felt as though he was abandoning Tommy, too, but knew he would be safe with the Robsons, and they would tell him where he'd gone. Tommy would understand.

Edward carried his tack to the field where Brandy grazed, saddled her and rode down the bank to Stotsfieldburn with Brown and Baker walking alongside. The carriage stood in the middle of the road. He tied the horse to the back, and they all climbed inside.

It was the same carriage he had ridden in all those years ago when he'd been taken to the orphanage. He had been totally enamoured with it then, but today, he was so anxious about the forthcoming encounter with his father that he hardly noticed it. He questioned the men further, but they knew no more than they had already told him. He fidgeted for the whole journey, trying to determine why his father wanted to speak with him.

It was late in the afternoon when the coach pulled up outside Granby Hall, and Lord Malham stood at the front door to meet them.

'Edward,' he said. 'I'm pleased to see that you're well, although you could do with a bath and some clean clothes. Go with Reynolds, and we'll talk at dinner.'

A wave of his father's hand sent the butler away to do his bidding, and Edward followed in his stead.

236

Reynolds led him to a large bedroom where servants ran around, filling a copper tub with hot water.

'Take a bath and I'll bring you some clothes. You're the same build as your father—that's good—I'll find something for you to wear. The drying cloths are on the ottoman at the foot of the bed.'

When the servants left the room, Edward undressed. He had never washed in a tub before, only with a cloth and water from a jug, or sometimes outdoors in a river. He stepped into the warm water, and it felt heavenly. Slowly, he lowered himself down until he was seated, took the soap and sponge in his hands, washed his body, and then lay back and washed his hair.

Reynolds returned with an outfit, laid it on the bed and left a razor and a bowl of water on a side table. 'A man will be along shortly to shave you,' he said before vacating the room.

Edward stepped out of the tub, dried himself on the linen cloth, and then dressed in the clothes that the butler had brought, thankful that they were not as garish as some of the outfits he'd seen Lord Malham wear.

A servant arrived and picked up the razor. Edward felt uncomfortable having someone else shave the stubble from his cheeks, chin and neck, but the man did a superb job, and he thanked him.

Once he was alone, Edward didn't know what to do. *Should I wait to be summoned to dinner or wander around the Hall until I stumble across the dining room?*

He decided that the polite option would be to wait. He looked out of one of the three windows in the large bedroom and admired the front garden, where he had first seen his father sitting with his wife. The vast lawns were surrounded

237

by shrubs, interspersed with mature trees—oak, beech and birch.

From his viewpoint, Edward could see the iron gates at the end of the drive, where the hound had bitten Tommy. Those gates had witnessed some of the most significant times in his life—when he first met his father and was sent to the orphanage when his father admitted there was no plan for his future and Edward had devised his own, as well as that dreadful night when the dog had mauled Tommy.

Edward wondered what Lord Malham would propose at dinner that evening and if it, too, might significantly affect his life.

Chapter 45

Reynolds knocked at the door, entered the room and looked Edward up and down. The smile on his face told Edward that the butler approved of what he saw.

'His Lordship requires your presence at his dinner table,' he said formally.

Edward turned from the window, still puzzling over why Lord Malham had sent Brown and Baker to track him down and deliver him to Granby Hall.

'Lead the way,' he said.

Edward followed the butler along the corridor and down the stairs to the large entrance hall, from which they took another passage to the dining room. The door was open, and Edward saw Lord Malham seated at the head of the table, sipping from a wine glass.

Reynolds led Edward to the other end of the long table, and he pulled out the chair for Edward to sit.

'No! Sit here, please.' Lord Malham pointed at the chair to his right.

Reynolds went to it and pulled it out so Edward could sit

next to his father, and when Edward was seated, the butler placed a napkin on his lap.

A servant girl carried a tray containing two bowls of soup, which she placed before them, and a second girl brought in some sliced bread on a tray and used silver tongs to put it on small plates on the table. Edward waited for his father to speak when the girls left the room.

'Eat, Edward,' said Lord Malham. 'You must be hungry. I know you haven't had anything to eat today.'

Edward was ravenous; he hadn't eaten since the evening meal with the Robsons the night before, and the vegetable soup before him smelled delicious. He picked up a slice of bread, dipped it into the soup, and took a large bite, earning a reprimanding look from Lord Malham, after which Edward ate more politely.

As soon as he finished the last mouthful and put down his spoon, the girls came in to clear away the dishes, brought back plates of beef with vegetables for their main course and filled the wine glasses with red wine.

'Burgundy,' said Lord Malham, twirling his glass so the liquid rolled around the sides. 'My favourite.'

Thinking he would have preferred a glass of ale with his meal, Edward tentatively took a sip of the wine and was pleasantly surprised. It was mellow and tasted far better than any wine he'd tried before, all of which he'd thought resembled vinegar. He understood now why his father savoured it.

'Thank you for coming here to speak with me today, Edward,' said Lord Malham.

'I had little say in the matter,' said Edward, remembering how he had been trapped and coerced into being there.

'I'm sorry for the method, but the circumstances required it.

Anyway, I would like to begin by apologising for my treatment of you in our earlier encounters.'

Edward was shocked to hear him say this, yet the man beside him looked sincere. There was none of the arrogance or jest that he had seen in the past. His father looked different. Serious. Older.

'Thank you,' Edward replied, accepting the apology. He could have ranted and raved about the injustice of spending five years in an orphanage, but what good would that have done either of them?

'Is that it?' Lord Malham raised his eyebrows. 'The young wretch that I was introduced to all those years ago would certainly have had a complaint.'

'I am not the boy that you met back then.'

'Indeed!' His father smiled at him, and he took another sip of wine. His face serious again, he said, 'You may have heard that my son, James, died in tragic circumstances.'

'Yes, sir, your men informed me. I'm sorry for your loss.'

'Thank you,' replied Lord Malham. 'Now, the reason I went to great lengths to find you is this. I am not getting any younger and I no longer have an heir to my estate. This is a heavy burden to me. I wondered if you would do me a great honour and become my legitimate son and heir?'

Edward shook his head. 'How can I be your legitimate son when you weren't married to my mother at the time of my conception?'

'My solicitors will see to that.'

'It could never work,' said Edward, leaning back in his chair and folding his arms. 'I understand you are aware that I'm a fugitive. I escaped from gaol, and there's a price on my head. If the constables discover I'm here, they'll arrest me. As your heir, your estate could be forfeit to the crown.'

Lord Malham laughed loudly. 'There's no need to worry about all that, Edward. Mere technicalities. I can have your charges lifted and you'll be able to live as freely as any other man, without fear of apprehension by the authorities. Of course, you would be welcome to live here at Granby Hall with me until the time came for you to inherit it.'

Edward ran his hands through his hair, his meal still untouched. Lord Malham was offering to be his father—a real father—and offering him a wonderful home that would eventually become his own. What else the Malham estate entailed, Edward didn't know, but he guessed it would include land, stock, worker's houses, and money.

If he accepted his father's offer, he would be a rich man and would be able to help many more children than ever before, but more than that, he could stay in England and take Dorothy as his wife.

How can I turn down such a life-changing offer?

After living outdoors for so long, with the constant threat of capture and the fear of imminent death, the promise of freedom and security was beyond belief.

'You sit and ponder,' said his father. 'I would love to know what's going on in that mind of yours.'

'How can I trust you?' asked Edward, looking his father in the eye. 'You've known that I was your son for years. When my mother died, you denied me a place in your family and sent me to an orphanage to be reared by strangers. When I came to you as a young man looking for your approval and direction, you laughed in my face. How do I know this time will be any different and that you won't change your mind?'

Edward's emotions were so confused that he didn't know if

242

he wanted to laugh, cry, punch the man, or hug him.

'Ah! A little of the boy remains, I see.' Lord Malham smiled ruefully. 'Circumstances have changed, Edward. I have changed,' he said emphatically. 'I was heartbroken when James died. I wished it had been me on that horse, trampled by the hunt, so that I wouldn't have had to suffer the loss and the grief of losing a son. I almost took my own life, so hard was it to bear.'

Lord Malham cleared his throat and took another sip of his wine before he could continue.

'My solicitor talked at length about inheritance. He insisted that I name a new heir and change my will accordingly, but I had no interest in such matters. Nothing seemed to matter at that time.'

'What changed?' asked Edward. 'Why did you send your men to find me?'

'I kept seeing you in my mind. You were there when I held a pistol to my head. It was the vision of you that stopped me from pulling the trigger. You know, you've troubled my thoughts since you arrived here as a boy. I sent you away because you reminded me of a wild past that I would rather forget.' Lord Malham spoke quietly and from the heart. 'I do remember your mother,' he confided. 'I should never have doubted your word. That's something I've regretted ever since.'

'Then, why didn't you make amends for it when I returned?' demanded Edward. 'I came to see you on my eighteenth birthday. You had the opportunity to put things right then. Don't you remember?'

'Yes, sadly I remember it well. You took me completely by surprise that day. I wanted to see you, so I came down to the entrance hall, but I had no idea what to say to you. You obviously thought I'd devised some grand scheme for you, but I hadn't, and I felt I'd let you down. I'm afraid my laughter was due to my embarrassment and lack of forethought. I should have made arrangements for you when you left that establishment. I'm sorry that I didn't think to do so. I am so sorry for how I acted towards you in our previous meetings. I hope you can forgive me and that we can start over.'

The old man's eyes were glassy as he looked at Edward.

'I accept your offer,' said Edward. His father had convinced him of his sincerity. 'I will be your son and heir, and it would be my honour, sir, but there is one condition.'

'Name it.' Lord Malham raised an eyebrow.

'That you use your influence to clear the name of my friend, Tommy Bell, too. He's been like a brother to me.'

'Consider it done.' Lord Malham took a sip of wine and replaced the glass on the table. Looking at Edward, he said, 'Is that all?'

Edward nodded and said, 'I believe so.'

'I have one request also.'

'Which is?' asked Edward.

'That you take my family name. Could you bear to be known as Edward Malham? Or perhaps Edward Earle-Malham?'

Edward swallowed. He had always been known as Edward Earle and was proud to bear his mother's name.

Can I take the name Malham from a man whom until today I held in little regard?

Since his father had offered him so much, clearing his and Tommy's names, giving them back their freedom, allowing them to stay in their own country, and making him his heir, he could meet that concession—it was a small price to pay.

'Yes, I believe I could endure the name Edward Earle-Malham, if that would please you, Lord Malham?'

'It would please me greatly, and it would please me even more if you would call me Father or Papa.'

'Thank you, Father.'

The men shook hands and smiled warmly at each other, gratified by their arrangement.

Chapter 46

Granby Hall, Durham
November 1770

The following day, Reynolds guided Edward to Lord Malham's study, an oak-panelled room with a large desk covered in green leather. Across it were strewn papers and documents.

His father looked up and said, 'Good morning, Edward! Please, sit down. Christopher will be here at any minute. I've had word from the stables that he's arrived.'

'Who is Christopher?' asked Edward, sitting opposite Lord Malham.

'My solicitor. He'll be dealing with all this,' he said, indicating the paperwork on the desk. 'There's my will, making you my legitimate son, your annuity payments, and sorting out the scrape that you and your friend got into.'

'The scrape?' said Edward, surprised at his father's choice of word. 'We would have been hanged if we hadn't escaped from gaol!'

'Well, we can call it whatever you like, Edward, but the fact is that young men have always gotten themselves into scrapes and fathers have always gotten them out of them. That's the way of the world.'

It was clear to Edward that his father had a very different perspective of the world than his own, and he guessed it was because he came from a privileged family. He was rapidly discovering the world was a very different place for the aristocracy.

'I can't thank you enough for sorting it out,' said Edward, still unable to believe that his father could have the charges dropped and their names cleared. He hadn't realised until they met the previous evening just how influential the man was.

'Believe me, your being here is thanks enough.'

A large man with sandy hair and a ruddy complexion opened the door and walked directly to Edward. Holding out his hand, he said, 'It's good to meet you at last, Edward. I've heard so much about you. Christopher Turner at your service.'

He sat next to Edward, put his bag on the floor, and rummaged through the papers on the desk.

'The first thing I need you to sign, Lord Malham, is the document that states Edward Earle is your son. I can complete the details.'

Lord Malham signed the paper and smiled at Edward. 'You are now officially my son.' He surprised Edward by coming around the table and kissing his cheek.

'Edward,' said Christopher, 'you need to sign this to take your father's name, and henceforth, you'll be known by the name Edward Earle-Malham.'

Edward signed the document, and when he looked up, his father was smiling at him proudly.

'And the next one is the amended will, which will make Edward your heir, sir,' said Christopher, placing another document before Lord Malham, which he signed.

'Now, to the annuity,' he continued efficiently. 'Have you decided how much you would like Edward to receive from the estate on an annual basis?'

'I have given it a great deal of thought, Christopher. He is to receive the same as my poor James—one thousand pounds a year.'

Edward's jaw dropped. 'But, sir—'

'There are no buts allowed today,' said his father. 'You'll want for nothing now that you're a Malham. Do you have a bank account?'

'No, sir, I've never needed one.'

'Can you open an account for Edward at the Durham branch, Christopher, and make the first payment as soon as possible?'

'Yes, sir. And finally, we need to consider the criminal charges against Edward and Thomas Bell. I believe the easiest way to resolve this matter would be for you, Lord Malham, to sign a document stating that Edward is your son and that he and his friend were in your company at Granby Hall on the night the alleged robbery occurred. The police will have no option but to drop the charges immediately as you are such a credible witness. Nobody would dare to doubt your word.'

'Excellent work, Christopher. You're worth every penny I pay you.'

'Thank you, sir,' said the solicitor as he gathered the papers from the desk, put them into his leather bag and left the room.

'I would love to know what you'll do with the money,' said Lord Malham, raising an eyebrow.

'Well, the first thing I'll do is get a headstone carved for my mother's grave. And then, I'll employ a thatcher to fix Tommy's roof. When it rains, it's almost as wet inside the cottage as it is outside. Also, I've been making regular donations to the orphanage in Sunderland for several years, but since I was arrested, I've been unable to give them any money. I'd like to make up for that.'

'All very noble causes,' said his father. 'Is there nothing that you'd like for yourself?'

Edward could think of only one thing he wanted.

'There is a young lady in Weardale that I intend to marry.'

The grin on his father's face shocked Edward. The man stood up, came around the table, and touched Edward's shoulder.

'My dear boy, you could not have made me happier,' he said. 'There's nothing more I would like to see before I leave this world than my grandchildren, another generation of Malhams to continue the line. It would be my pleasure to pay for your upcoming marriage and wedding reception, which will be held here at the Hall. Just name the date.'

'Thank you,' said Edward, and nervously added, 'All I need to do now is ask her if she'll have me.'

Lord Malham's head went back, and he roared with laughter. When he regained control, he said, 'Return to Weardale right away and propose to the young lady, and put yourself out of your misery one way or the other. I'm sure you're worrying for nothing.'

Edward hoped his father was right. So much had changed since Dorothy had wanted to flee the country with him.

Would she want to marry into the gentry?

For that was what all of this paperwork had made him—a member of the aristocracy. It was a gigantic leap from eloping with Edward Earle, clerk and highwayman, to marrying Edward Earle-Malham, son and heir to Lord Malham of Granby Hall.

'I will do that, sir. Thank you again for everything that you've done for me and Tommy.'

'It's too little, too late, in my opinion Edward, and I apologise for that. I hope I can make it up to you.'

Edward left Granby Hall and rode to Rookhope, arriving at dusk. As he approached the farmhouse door, it swung open. Dorothy stood there for a second and then ran into his arms, and he held her tightly, feeling her sobbing against his chest.

'It's alright, Dorothy, I'm back,' he said, holding her head. 'Everything is alright.'

She looked at him with teary eyes and said, 'I thought I'd lost you! I woke up, intending to run away with you, and you'd gone!'

'Come over here and sit down,' said Edward. 'There's so much I need to tell you.'

They sat on the bench in the farmyard, and Edward recounted the story of the past few days.

Dorothy lifted her hand to his cheek and said, 'I'm pleased that you're on good terms with your father. Family is so important and you haven't had one for such a long time.'

That was typical of Dorothy, he thought. She wasn't impressed by the wealth and status he had suddenly acquired; she was more concerned about his relationship with his father. And she was right. He had needed a family for so long, and now he had one.

That should have been enough, but looking at Dorothy, he wanted more. He wanted a wife and children of his own, a house full of children like the Robsons had had.

He got down on one knee and said, 'Dorothy, will you marry me?'

Dorothy leapt up from the seat and stared at him.

'Are you being serious?' she asked, her eyes wide.

'Yes, Dorothy, I've never been more serious in my life. I've always loved you and I want you to be my wife.'

'Of course, I will. I thought you'd never ask!' she said, jumping into his arms. 'There's never been anyone in my heart but you.'

They kissed passionately, and then he held her close, ecstatically happy, unable to believe he would finally marry his Dorothy.

'We should tell your parents,' he said, taking her hand.

The couple entered the house, their joined hands and smiles giving away their news before they could open their mouths.

Mrs Robson moved over to her daughter and opened her arms. She hugged Dorothy and then Edward.

'Congratulations! I knew you two would get together someday. I'm so happy for you both.'

She wiped away her tears.

Edward addressed Mr Robson, who sat quietly by the fire, watching the proceedings.

'Mr Robson, I apologise. I should have asked your permission for your daughter's hand in marriage before I asked her to be my wife. I hope we have your blessing.'

The old man rose to his feet and looked Edward in the eye.

'Aye, if that's what she wants, you have it.'

Her father looked at Dorothy, and she nodded, smiling broadly.

'Just treat her right and make her happy,' he said.

'I will,' said Edward. 'I promise.'

Mr Robson shook Edward's hand, kissed his daughter's cheek, and then hugged his wife.

Tommy came through the door and said, 'Edward, you're

back! What's going on? Is everythin' alright?'

'Yes, things couldn't be any better. Dorothy and I are to be married!'

'That's great news, but how—'

'Sit down, Tommy, and I'll tell you everything.'

Tommy sat at the kitchen table, and Edward and Dorothy sat opposite him.

Edward told Tommy about the visit to his father, their agreement and the change in their circumstances.

'So, it's all over?' asked Tommy bewildered.

'Yes, it's all over. We're safe now. We can put our past behind us and move on.'

'I can't believe it. Does that mean we can go home?'

'It might be better if you come back to Granby Hall with me and stay there for a few days until everything is settled, and then you can go home and do whatever you want.'

Tommy sighed loudly, shook his head and smiled.

Edward knew precisely how Tommy felt. The relief that they were no longer being hunted and their lives were no longer in jeopardy was immense.

Chapter 47

Granby Hall, Durham
June 1771

The morning was bright and clear as the servants at Granby Hall prepared to receive upward of two hundred guests for the largest party held there since the first marriage of the present Lord Malham thirty-one years earlier.

A valet helped Edward dress for his wedding while Tommy stood by the window, giving a running commentary on the activities at the front of the house.

'They're carrying tables out now and setting them up on the lawn.'

'Never mind that,' said Edward. 'Do you have the ring?'

'Of course, I have. I wouldn't be a very good groomsman if I forgot that, would I?' Tommy felt his coat pocket to be sure.

The valet helped Edward into his coat and stepped back to admire his handiwork. 'Very good, sir. You're ready.'

'The coach is pullin' up in front of the house now,' said Tommy. 'Come on. We should go down. I can't wait to have a ride in it.'

At the bottom of the staircase, Edward noticed the newly painted portrait of himself hanging in the entrance hall, fitting in perfectly with the other family pictures as he'd predicted years ago. He had never imagined he'd see it hanging there alongside his father's.

As Edward and Tommy rode in the luxurious coach to Durham Cathedral, Edward couldn't believe the change in their fortunes. Only six months ago, they had been fugitives from the law, with a price on their heads, sleeping rough, and now they were free men. Edward lived in one of the most beautiful houses in the county and received an extremely generous annuity from his father. And he was about to marry the woman he loved.

Can life get any better than this?

The carriage climbed the steep bank towards Palace Green, passed the entrance to Durham Gaol, and stopped outside the magnificent Norman Cathedral.

The men climbed down and faced each other.

'How do I look?' asked Edward.

'Very smart,' said Tommy. 'But then you usually do.'

They walked to the front pew and sat down to await the bride's arrival.

Around ten minutes later, the Bishop of Durham, standing by the altar, raised his hands for the groom and groomsman to stand. The choir began to sing, and Edward looked down the aisle at the most beautiful woman he had ever seen. She was walking towards him with a serene smile, wearing a slim-fitting cream dress with a low neckline, her strawberry blonde hair flowing loosely down her back, and she carried a bouquet of lavender.

The familiar scent reminded Edward of home.

Edward's heart skipped a beat when his bride-to-be stopped by his side and looked up into his eyes.

The Bishop performed the marriage rites with a flourish, and within half an hour, he pronounced the couple man and wife.

After kissing her, Edward took Dorothy's hand. They walked down the aisle with huge grins on their faces and climbed into the waiting carriage by the door.

A long line of carriages, coaches, carts and riding horses followed them from Durham to Granby Hall for the wedding reception.

Outside the Hall, the indoor and outdoor staff stood in neat lines to welcome Lord Malham's daughter-in-law, the future Lady of Granby Hall, to her new home.

Edward helped Dorothy climb down the steps from the carriage and walked up and down the rows, speaking with every one of them. Then, to everybody's delight, Edward picked up his bride, carried her up the steps and through the front door, and lowered her to her feet in the large entrance hall. He could not resist kissing her.

'There's plenty of time for that later,' said Lord Malham, smirking as he walked through the door with his fourth wife. 'Let's eat, drink and have fun!'

The grand hall had two long tables down the sides and one along the top edge, with white tablecloths, silver candelabras, and floral decorations of roses, peonies and poppies. The cutlery was all silver, and it had been polished for the occa-sion, and the crystal wine and water glasses sparkled in the flickering candlelight.

'It's perfect,' said Dorothy as she sat by Edward's side at the centre of the top table.

'You're perfect,' he said, gently kissing the end of her nose.

Lord Malham spared no expense on the marriage of his son

and heir. After a delicious five-course meal, the guests were invited outside to mingle on the lawns and offered drinks of their choosing. The finest wines, sherries, brandies, whiskies and teas flowed freely in the grounds of Granby Hall.

Edward spotted John Robson with his wife and young son in the crowd, and he and Dorothy made their way over to them.

'John, Jenny, how are you?' he asked.

The Robsons congratulated the newlywed couple, and John hugged his sister and then his friend.

Dorothy asked Jenny about her nephew, and while the ladies were distracted, John said, 'I don't suppose you'll have any more silver for me now that you've landed on your feet.'

'No,' replied Edward. 'But if you were relying on the income from it, I can help you out.'

'No need for that,' John said smugly. 'I've had a promotion. You're lookin' at the new manager of the Nenthead Lead Smelting Mill.'

'How did that happen?' asked Edward.

'The company was so impressed with the process I'd invented for gettin' the silver out of the ore that they dismissed Beattie and asked me to take his place.'

'Good for you!' said Edward, genuinely happy for his friend. 'You will come and visit us, won't you? We have plenty of space to accommodate you.'

Looking at the mansion, they laughed, and John promised that he and his family would keep in touch.

Edward saw Alexander Dunsmore standing with his wife, admiring the gardens, and he walked through the crowd to the edge of the lawn.

'Mr Dunsmore,' he said, 'I'm glad you could come.'

'I wouldnae have missed it for the world,' said the Scotsman. 'I love a good weddin'.'

'I understand your sister-in-law has been married recently,' said Edward.

'Aye, our Charlotte's made a good match. She married Laird Jamie Drummond in April. A respectable family and one that can afford to indulge her shoppin' habit.'

Edward smiled knowingly. He had met Charlotte in town numerous times, and she'd always had boxes and packages for him to carry.

'Please pass on my regards to them,' he said.

'I feel foolish that I didnae ken you were Lord Malham's son. I should have guessed 'cos you're the exact likeness of yer father. I've met him before at a few charity events.'

Edward knew Dunsmore was unaware of his past criminal activities or that, until recently, he had been the bastard son of Lord Malham. His father had done as he'd promised; he was now a legitimate son and heir to the Lord, and he'd been cleared of his crimes. That life was well and truly behind him.

'Yes, so I've been told. No doubt you'll be delighted to hear my wife and I intend to continue to contribute to your orphanage and to increase our patronage to many more in the region too.'

'That's verra kind of you both, and it's appreciated, I can tell ya. On behalf of the weans, please accept my sincerest thanks.'

Looking around, Edward said, 'If you'll excuse me, there are some people I need to see before they leave.'

Edward was shocked to see Tommy standing near the drive with Sarah Potts and curious as to why she had come to his wedding.

'Sarah, what a surprise,' he said coldly. 'I didn't expect to see you here.'

'You said I could bring a guest, Edward,' said Tommy. 'I didn't think you'd mind.'

'I didn't expect you to bring a traitor, Tommy. I thought you had more sense than that.'

'It wasn't Sarah that told on us!' exclaimed Tommy, putting an arm around her protectively. 'I don't know why you think it was.'

Edward noticed the gesture and wondered how close Tommy and Sarah had become—they were most definitely a courting couple.

'Was it you who told the police that we were highwaymen and sent them to our door?' Edward asked Sarah directly.

'No, I didn't say anythin' to the constables. I would never have done that.'

Sincerity shone from her eyes, and Edward's brow furrowed.

'But you changed towards me. You clearly disapproved of my association with Charlotte Liddell. I thought that perhaps—'

'You've got it all wrong, Edward,' said Sarah. 'I was concerned about you, no more than that. I overheard Mr Dunsmore talkin' and I knew that he intended to palm Miss Liddell off onto a wealthy man, and he'd set his sights on you. It was no accident that she was at the orphanage when you were there—it was all planned. She never came at any other time. Anyway, I was upset about them using you and concerned that if you and Miss Liddell became close, she might discover your secret.'

'If it wasn't you, then who was it?' asked Edward, perplexed. 'Nobody else knew what we did and where we lived.'

'Someone else knew where you lived,' said Sarah, looking down at her feet. 'I'm very sorry if I did wrong and caused you harm, but Miss Liddell came to me and said that she needed to see you urgently, that she was madly in love with you, and had to tell you before you married someone else. I wasn't sure what to do. I didn't know if you were keen on her or not, but you always looked happy in her company. I'm so sorry, Edward, I told her where you lived. I believe it was Charlotte who told the police.'

'Charlotte! Streuth!'

Edward ran his hands over his hair. He would never have suspected Charlotte of betraying him in a million years. When he'd spurned her advances and told her he was promised to another woman, a white lie at the time, she must have been so consumed with jealousy that she'd wanted revenge. It appeared she had deliberately set out to cause him trouble.

But how did she know I was a highwayman?

He was sure there was no way she could have known he was a highwayman. The only solution he could think of was that she had read the description of the highwayman seen at the accident near Chester-le-Street. The report in the newspaper had been remarkably precise regarding his height, build and colouring.

He guessed that she had reported him to the police as an act of mischief meant to inconvenience him rather than as an act of malice with intent to endanger his life, but whichever, she had either wittingly or unwittingly put his and Tommy's lives in grave danger. The time between their arrest and the meeting with his father at Granby Hall had been an absolute nightmare, but at least they had survived. The whole episode could have ended very differently.

It was no wonder Charlotte had fled to Scotland after she had given the police the identity and whereabouts of the highwayman they sought. He hoped she regretted her actions and felt dreadful when she learned of his arrest. He and Tommy had come so close to losing their lives because of her foolish prank or malicious act.

He hoped he never set eyes on Miss Charlotte Liddell again because, at that moment, he wanted to strangle her for what she'd put them through.

'Never mind, Sarah,' he said calmly despite his overactive mind. 'It all worked out well in the end. I'm very sorry that I doubted your loyalty.'

He leaned forward and kissed her cheek.

'Edward!' said Lord Malham, 'You've only been married a few hours and already I find you kissing another lady.' Lord Malham laughed loudly.

'Father, may I present Miss Sarah Potts. Sarah this is my father, Lord Edward Malham.'

Lord Malham stepped closer and said, 'Potts, did you say?'

'Yes, Miss Sarah Potts,' Edward confirmed.

'Young lady, you are the image of a woman I once knew. She was a Potts, too. Emily Potts.'

Edward saw Sarah's smile fall from her lips and her brows draw together. 'My mother was called Emily Potts, sir.'

'Oh, I'm sorry. Is she no longer with us?'

'I don't know. She abandoned me when I was a baby.'

Edward looked again at Sarah's green eyes and took a step back at the same time as his father did.

'Blazes!' said Lord Malham, looking at Edward.

'What's wrong?' asked Tommy, puzzled by their reactions.

'If I'm right, I believe Sarah is my half-sister,' said Edward, looking at Lord Malham for confirmation.

'I think you may be correct in that assumption.'

Sarah looked rapidly from one to the other. 'You mean you're my father?' she asked Lord Malham, 'and Edward's my brother.'

'Yes, I believe that is so,' said Lord Malham. 'I had no idea Emily had a child. She simply disappeared from my life. You said your mother abandoned you? Who cared for you? Where did you live?'

Lowering her face, she said, 'At the orphanage in Sunderland, sir. I still live and work there.'

'Oh, no! I'm so sorry, my dear,' said Lord Malham. 'You'll not work there or stay there another day. You must come and stay with us.'

'But, sir—'

'She's very much like you, Edward,' said Lord Malham, smiling. 'Sarah, you're a Malham now, and as your father, I'm asking you to live here with your family—that's myself, my wife, Henrietta, Edward and Dorothy—and I would like you to call me Father rather than sir. Now, what do you say?'

Sarah looked at Edward for direction, and he nodded and grinned at her.

'Alright, sir—Father. Thank you!'

Edward hugged Sarah and whispered, 'It feels so good to have a family, doesn't it?'

She nodded at him, smiling widely, tears of joy in her eyes.

'Having Edward here as my son has brought me so much joy,' said Lord Malham. 'I've never had a daughter before and I'm absolutely delighted to have found you. Why don't we go inside and have a little chat?' he asked, offering her his arm. 'I'd love to get to know you better and I'll tell you all I know about your mother. Emily was such a pretty young woman, just like you.'

Edward bade Sarah and Tommy farewell and watched them walk with his father towards the house. He looked around the grounds, saw Dorothy standing with her family in the middle of the gathering, and walked over to join them. He suspected they'd been discussing him because they fell silent when he reached them.

'What have I interrupted?' he asked, putting his arm around Dorothy's waist and pulling her to his side.

Mr Robson cleared his throat. 'I was just tellin' this lot about the last time I came here. After that day, when I brought you to meet your father, I never wanted to set eyes on this place again. It broke me heart leavin' you here with him, knowin' what he intended for you. And now here we are, celebratin' your marriage to our Dot, and this will be your home. Who would have thought it?'

Mr Robson hugged Edward firmly and said, 'I'm proud to have you as a son-in-law, Ed, but you've always been a part of our family, you know that.'

Edward wiped away a tear from his eye. After being alone for so long, he now belonged to two families and had never been happier.

'Thank you, Mr Robson.'

'No more of that Mr Robson nonsense. You can call me John or Father if you want—I don't mind which.'

'Thank you, Father,' he said. He'd wanted to call Mr Robson father for so long that it rolled off his tongue like he'd been saying it for years.

As the Robsons made to leave, Jimmy winked conspiratorially at Edward and shook his hand. Edward was so grateful that Jimmy helped him and Tommy escape from the gaol; he would forever be in his debt. Without his assistance, Edward was sure that he and Tommy would have been tried for highway robbery and hanged. Edward and his father would never have been reconciled; he would never have known he had a sister, nor would he have married his childhood sweetheart. And Tommy wouldn't have had the opportunity to court Sarah and maybe, in time, become his brother-in-law.

As most of the guests Edward knew had left the reception, he took Dorothy's hand, and they returned to the house, their new home, Granby Hall.

Author's Historical Note

I thoroughly enjoyed researching and writing this novel. The story of Edward Earle and its characters are entirely fictional, but the title character was inspired by a real-life highwayman I read about in some old newspaper articles dating from the 1770s.

His name was John Collingwood, and he was born at Rookhope in County Durham, England, the village where I was born and grew up. He operated as a highwayman in Northern England on the Newcastle and Sunderland turnpike roads.

Being a highwayman in the eighteenth century was a risky undertaking. Two years earlier, Robert Hazlett robbed the Newcastle and Durham mail coach. He was caught and convicted for the crime, executed at the gallows in Durham, and his body hung in chains (gibbeted) on Gateshead Fell. Being hung in chains was usually reserved for the most serious offenders—murderers or traitors. Robbing a mail coach was considered one of the most severe crimes then, but the fact that Hazlett had stolen from the judge who presided over his trial may have influenced the outcome of his case.

Before the days of photography, detailed descriptions of criminals were essential for the police to identify suspects, and these descriptions were used in newspaper reports about wanted criminals and escaped convicts.

John Collingwood was described as about twenty-five years of age, about five feet eight inches tall, of a black complexion, thin visage, his face much beaten by the weather, remarkably hairy in his body, and with dark brown short hair curled towards the ends, sometimes worn tied at the back with a black ribbon. He was said to be wide-kneed and to walk wide upon his legs, stooping and wriggling when he moved.

His walking difficulties may have been due to a congenital disability, bone fractures that had healed incorrectly, or rickets caused by a dietary deficiency in vitamin D. Collingwood is described as having a black complexion in one description and swarthy in another, and it is known he worked underground in coal mines. As vitamin D is absorbed through the skin from sunlight, rickets is a likely cause.

In the early 1770s, Collingwood had two accomplices. John Armstrong from Middleton-in-Teesdale had worked as a lead miner until a month earlier when he went to Sunderland and became a caster of keels. He was thirty years of age, badly marked by smallpox and blind in his left eye. The other accomplice was John Oxley from Swalwell, a skipper of a keel at Sunderland with a tall and stout build. He had dimples on his chin and nose and a blemish on the left side of his head caused by scalding when he was a child. When these three men were together, they would have been unmistakable.

The police captured Armstrong and Oxley in November 1772. The prisoners were incarcerated in Durham Gaol. A newspaper notice read, 'Whoever can charge the said John Armstrong and John Oxley or either of them, with any crime or misdemeanour, they may have an opportunity of seeing them.' John Collingwood was still at large at this time and was thought to have gone towards Whitby or Scarborough, which suggests he got away on a boat and headed south down the coast.

The following year, John Collingwood was captured too, but a headline on the 10th of April was 'Escaped from Justice'. After his escape, there were sightings of Collingwood at Wolsingham and Witton-le-Wear in County Durham and Alston in Cumberland, and he usually rode a chestnut or grey mare. A reward of ten guineas was offered to anyone who would apprehend Collingwood so that he could be secured in any of His Majesty's goals.

Collingwood was apprehended six years later, in 1779 and taken to Carlisle Gaol. He had been recognised at Seaton, near Whitehaven in Cumberland, where he worked as a collier. By this time, he was wanted for stealing at least five horses from Westgate, Lanchester and Hexham and also for house-breaking at Capheaton, where he climbed down a chimney, broke an elderly woman's arm and stole seven shillings in silver.

At the Carlisle Assizes that summer, it was decided that Collingwood was to remain in gaol. Another man accused of horse stealing at the same court was found guilty and sentenced to death but was reprieved.

Collingwood stayed in Carlisle Gaol until July 1780, when a gaoler came to take him to stand trial in Durham.

At the time of writing, I have been unable to find out what happened to John Collingwood after he was transferred to Durham. However, a newspaper article dated 1783 states a man named Collingwood was arrested at Whitehaven and taken to Carlisle Gaol on suspicion of horse stealing. If this is the same man, it appears that Collingwood either didn't make it to Durham Gaol three years earlier or managed to escape from custody again. It is unlikely that he stood trial and was acquitted when there were so many charges against him.

The records are sketchy, but his name does not appear on the list of men hanged at Durham.

With confirmed sightings and a high price on his head, one wonders why he was not betrayed. Did the people of Weardale shield him? Were they benefiting in some way from his crimes? Did they live in fear of the man? Or did the Weardale people resent the authorities so much that they were unwilling to help?

Despite John Collingwood being the original inspiration for this story,

The idea for melting down silver at a lead smelting mill came about because galena, the lead ore found in the North Pennines, has a small amount of silver occurring naturally within it. The silver was separated and removed during the lead smelting process. Ore from different lead mines produced different percentages of silver; some contained significantly higher quantities than others. I don't believe that the smelting mills at Nenthead and Rookhope were used for melting down stolen silver, but they would have been the ideal place to do so.

About the Author

Best-selling author, Margaret Manchester studied local history and archaeology at the University of Durham, and was awarded a Master's degree in Archaeology, and then taught archaeology, local history and genealogy. Margaret was born in Weardale, County Durham, England. She had a strong interest in family history from a young age, and discovered many of her ancestors had lived and worked in the area for centuries, either as lead miners, smelters or farmers.

Margaret still lives in County Durham with her husband. As well as writing, she is currently a director of an award-winning business and a charity trustee at the Weardale Museum. She enjoys spending time in her garden and with her dogs.

You can connect with me on:

🌐 https://www.margaretmanchester.com

🐦 https://twitter.com/m_r_manchester

📘 https://www.facebook.com/margaretmanchesterauthor

🔗 https://www.instagram.com/margaret_manchester

Also by Margaret Manchester

The Lead Miner's Daughter
Amazon #1 International Bestseller

Northern England, 1872. Mary Watson, a lead miner's daughter, leaves her childhood home to work at Springbank Farm. She soon meets a handsome neighbour, Joe Milburn, and becomes infatuated with him, but is he the right man for her?

Mary's story is woven into a background of rural life and crime in the remote valley of Weardale. Not one but two murders shock the small community.

Find yourself in the farmhouse kitchen with the Peart family, walking on the wide-open fells, seeking shelter underground and solving crimes with PC Emerson as this intriguing story unfolds.

Will the culprits be brought to justice? And will Mary find true love?

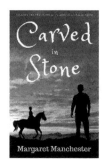

Carved in Stone

Amazon #1 UK Bestseller

Northern England, 1881. Sent away during her brother's trial, Phyllis Forster returns home after a seven-year absence to find the Weardale people have turned against the Forster family and she desperately wants to win back their respect. Can trust and harmony be restored in this rural community?

At twenty-eight years of age, she has almost given up hope of love and marriage, and throws herself into the management of the family estate, until two very different men come into her life.

Ben, troubled by the past and full of anger and distrust, is a shepherd who shuns the company of others until his new boss arrives at Burnside Hall.

Timothy, the new vicar, is preoccupied with the ancient past, but he takes a keen interest in Phyllis.

Will she settle for just a husband? Or will she defy convention and follow her heart?

Fractured Crystal

Northern England, 1895. Josie Milburn meets Elliott Dawson, a man who shares her interest in collecting crystals. Defying an age-old superstition, Elliott takes Josie into a lead mine, an action that sets off a sequence of dramatic events, beginning with a miner's death the same day.

Elliott and Josie face a series of trials involving tragic loss and the unveiling of family secrets, which change their lives and fortunes in ways that they could never have imagined.

Will these traumatic circumstances bind them together or break them apart?

Briar Place

Northern England 1849. A dispute between the lead miners and Mr Sopwith brings about a strike with disastrous consequences. Loyalties are tested, blacklegs punished and families divided.

At Briar Place, the Dixon and Lowery families were friends and neighbours, but not anymore. Jack and Bella are caught in their feud. Will their relationship end in heartbreak or can love conquer all?

When the repercussions of the strike finally come to an end, seventeen-year-old Lizzie Lowery is left to pick up the pieces.

A compelling family saga set during the historic miners' strike at Allenheads in 1849.

Printed by Amazon Italia Logistica S.r.l.
Torrazza Piemonte (TO), Italy

59806293R00159